CALLY &JIMMY

TWINS TOGETHER

ZOE ANTONIADES

ILLUSTRATED BY **KATIE KEAR**

ANDERSEN PRESS

For George Hendle

First published in 2022 by
Andersen Press Limited
20 Vauxhall Bridge Road, London, SW1V 2SA, UK
Vijverlaan 48, 3062 HL Rotterdam, Nederland
www.andersenpress.co.uk

2 4 6 8 10 9 7 5 3 1

British Library Cataloguing in Publication Data available.

ISBN 978 1 83913 128 8

Printed and bound in Great Britain
by Clays Ltd, Elcograf S.p.A..

CALLY & JIMMY

TWINS TOGETHER

Also in this series:

What's it like being a twin? Well, it's kind of a cool thing because people find it really interesting and a bit special. And it *would* be cool and special and it probably *is* for lots of *other* twins, but if your twin's anything like my twin Jimmy, then it can also be totally annoying.

Twins get compared to each other a lot. But there's no point doing that with me and Jimmy cos we're completely different. I don't want to sound big-headed or anything, but I'm sensible and he's silly. At school, I sit at the 'top table' but he has to be at the front with his teaching assistant, Miss Loretta. I'm given responsibilities and get to be independent, when Jimmy, well, he just gets all the attention.

To be fair to Jimmy, he's still good at lots of things, like running and gaming and using his imagination and making people laugh, and it's not all his fault that he finds some of the other stuff more difficult. He's got ADHD which makes it harder for him to stay focused, and so things like being calm, following the rules and passing tests don't come so easily to him. I'd feel sorry for him if only he didn't keep messing everything up for me too. Cos I'm his twin. And twins have to be in it together. So, whenever there's trouble for Jimmy, somehow there ends up being trouble for me too. Double trouble, that's what being twins is. Like the time when we really wanted to take our class's pet hamster home for half term . . .

Our class's pet hamster is called Lightning.

4

Mrs Wright got him for us at the beginning of Year Five. As soon as she introduced him to everyone, he bolted onto his hamster wheel and started racing about on it at a million miles per hour.

'Whoa. He's well speedy!'

'Watch him go!'

'Like lightning!'

And that's how Lightning got his name.

When it gets to be the school holidays, someone in the class is allowed to take Lightning home to look after him. Half term break was coming up, and at home time, just before we'd got all our bags and coats, Mrs Wright made her end-of-the-day announcements.

5

'We need to start getting ideas together for our charity fundraiser, so get your thinking caps on and see what you can come up with . . .'

Last term's bake sale hadn't gone according to plan, especially when Jimmy ended up pushing me headfirst into the entire table display sending everything flying and leaving me covered in icing sugar and buttercream. But that's another story.

'And anyone who hasn't returned their parents' evening slips needs to get those back to me ASAP – ' Mrs Wright glared at Mitch Moran and Jackson Boyle – 'that means "As Soon As Possible" to you two, not next Christmas, thank you very much.'

Jimmy couldn't help himself from sniggering and Mitch Moran muttered under his breath, 'At least the teachers will have something decent to say about me, not like you, Dimmy.'

'What was that you said, Mitch?' asked Mrs Wright.

Mrs Wright might not have heard him exactly. But Jimmy had. I could tell, because his ears had gone red.

'Nothing, Miss. Just, like, I'll get my mum to sign the letter, Miss,' Mitch shrugged.

I'd already got my parents' evening reply slip in. I was one of the first. Like I said, I'm responsible. Anyway, I have to be, cos sorting out the parents' evening appointments is a bit tricky in our family as Mum and Dad aren't together any more. They still get on OK though. They don't row all the time like Lauren

Bennett's parents or anything. In fact, Mum and Dad both usually come to all the school things, special assemblies and sports days and all. It just takes a bit more organising sometimes; like with parents' evening, you need to get the right time-slot before they all get snapped up.

Mrs Wright continued, 'And as half term is coming up, we need to see who'd like to take Lightning home to look after.'

Everyone put up their hands and cried, 'Me, me, me!' standing on their toes to see who could get their hand up the highest. Jimmy was doing that thing where he puts one hand under his other elbow so he can push his arm higher than anyone else's.

Mrs Wright rolled her eyes and laughed, 'Let me rephrase that. We need to see whose *parents* would be willing to have Lightning over the half term.'

That ruled us out then. Mum's never had time for pets. She says she's too busy.

And as for Yiayia, that's our Greek granny from Cyprus who lives with us, she thinks hamsters are pests. Me and Jimmy showed her pictures of some on the internet when our class first got Lightning and she couldn't believe it.

'What is this things? This things is pet? Is like mouse. Is like rat. This things is live where is the dustbin outside, not in house!' In Yiayia's opinion, all animals belong outside. That's how it is in Cyprus anyway. Like at Aunty Maria's house in Deftera – they keep their dog Hari in a kennel and they have chickens in the yard. But there was no way we could have Lightning outside. He'd freeze.

We wouldn't be able to keep Lightning at Dad's either because we only stay with him every other weekend. And his flat's too far away. In Clapham. It's still London, but London's big and there's loads of traffic, so it takes forever to get there.

But when Yiayia came to pick us up from

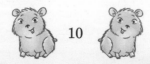

school, Jimmy tried his luck anyway. He flew across the playground over to Yiayia and started bouncing around like Tigger times two-hundred. 'Yiayia, Yiayia, can we have Lightning for half term? Please, please, please, please, please?'

'What is you talking about, Jimmy mou?' asked Yiayia, scrabbling in her bag for our after-school snacks and pulling out two spanakopita wrapped in kitchen towel.

'He means our class's pet hamster,' I explained. 'You know. Like the ones I showed you pictures of. Someone always gets to take him home in the school holidays.'

'Oh no, no, no, no, no,' said Yiayia, making the sign of the cross (a sort of prayer thing old lady Greek people do all the time). 'Is every time you ask this, isn't it?'

We'd been through this before. At autumn half term and Christmas too. Now Yiayia realised what Jimmy was going on about, she wasn't having any of it. Yiayia usually is the one who spoils Jimmy the most, she's the one who always gives in to him, especially when he does this puppy-eyed thing that always works with Yiayia, cos Jimmy's secretly her favourite, even though you're not meant to have favourites with twins. But this time, all the pleading in the world would not make Yiayia cave in. This time 'no' really meant 'no'.

'Is like mouse. Is like rat. This things is live where is the dustbin outside, not in house,' she reminded us. Then she took each of us by the hand and marched us home. Jimmy sulked the whole way.

He was still miserable when we got in. He stayed that way all evening. When we were watching TV, he just stared at it and didn't even laugh at his favourite programmes. He huffed

12

and puffed through his homework (but to be honest, he always does that). And his face was like thunder when he played on his tablet, even though he loves StreetBrix.

When it was dinner time and Mum had got back from work and joined us at the table, she looked at Jimmy and sighed, 'Why the long face?'

Jimmy was in such a mood, all he could say was, 'Hmph!'

Mum looked to me for answers. As usual.

'Mrs Wright asked who wanted to bring Lightning home for half term, and we reaaaaalllly want to,' I said.

Mum put her hand to her head and groaned, 'Oh, not that daft hamster again.'

That's when Jimmy snapped out of his silent fury and exploded. Slamming his fists on the table, he yelled, 'He's not daft. He's the best. Why can't we have him? It's not fair.'

Yiayia made the sign of the cross and looked to the heavens.

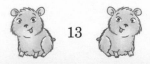

'Now, calm down, Jimmy,' said Mum. 'We've been through this before. I've got enough to do without having to worry about pets as well.'

'But you won't have to do anything, Mum,' I pleaded. 'We can look after it. We're ten now. We can be responsible. We'll clean out the cage and feed him and fill up his water bottle and everything.'

Mum looked at Jimmy. We all knew there was no 'we' about it. If we were to get a pet, the responsibility of looking after it would be all mine. But that was OK. I like responsibility. The teachers always choose me for jobs at school.

'Please, Mum,' I begged. 'I can look after Lightning. I know I can.'

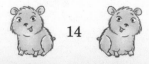

14

And then . . . I couldn't believe it . . . but it really did look like Mum was softening. Yiayia noticed it too because she started shaking her head and saying, 'Mana mou, mana mou.'

Jimmy clasped his hands under his chin and looked up at Mum with his puppy eyes. It's amazing how he can go from face-of-thunder to Mr Angelic in the space of ten seconds. 'Please, please, please, please, please, please, Mum. I'll love you forever, my bestest bestest Mum in the whole entire universe.'

Mum looked at Yiayia who threw her hands up in the air in defeat. 'Is still like mouse. Is still like rat. Is still should to be live in dustbin.'

Mum actually chuckled a bit at that, 'Oh come on, Mama. They're not so bad. They're domestic. They're really quite clean. They wouldn't allow them in the classroom if they weren't.'

Yiayia folded her arms. She had nothing more to say on the matter.

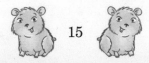

Now me and Jimmy were both gazing at Mum and saying, 'Please, please, please, please, please . . .' over and over again.

'Oh . . . well . . . OK . . . I suppose . . . What harm could it really do?' Mum smiled.

Me and Jimmy both leaped out of our seats and cheered, 'Yesssssssssssss!'

Jimmy danced about the kitchen then did a lap of victory around the living room and cartwheeled back over to the dining table. I ran over to Mum and gave her the biggest hug and said, 'Mum, you really are the best.'

Yiayia just gave a little snort. 'Come on, everybody. Eat. Eat. Is dinner is getting cold.'

★

Mum had to write a letter to school to say we were interested in taking Lightning home with us, and then we had to wait till the middle of the next week for Mrs Wright to make her decision. To us it felt like having to wait forever. Three other children in our class had asked for permission too, so it could have been any of us.

'I'm gonna keep my fingers crossed the whole time until Mrs Wright chooses,' said Jimmy. I didn't think he actually meant it. It was a bit extreme. But then Jimmy *is* extreme. And when it came to Lightning, he was obsessed. So that's what he did. Whenever I looked at him, he had his fingers crossed – at breakfast, at school, when he was riding his bike, he even said he kept them crossed under his pillow at night. And when the time came for Mrs Wright to make her announcement, we both had absolutely everything crossed.

It was towards the end of the day on Wednesday. We were all sitting on the carpet and Mrs Wright had just finished reading to us from our Book of the Week. She makes sure we always have story time and it's my favourite part of lessons. Jimmy was on his own special cushion by Mrs Wright's feet. I was at the back with my best friend Aisha. Because we're both sensible, we can sit where we want. We don't need to be kept an eye on. Aisha whispered to me, 'Hope it's you.' She isn't allowed any pets. Her parents are a bit like Yiayia when it comes to having animals inside. But I'd promised her that if we did get to take Lightning home, she could come round to our house as much as she liked to play with him and help with feeding him and cleaning out the cage and everything.

'So . . .' said Mrs Wright.

The suspense was killing me.

'The children I have chosen to take Lightning home are . . .'

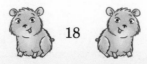

Children! She said children! It had to be us then. Cos we're twins and there are two of us. Jimmy hadn't cottoned on yet. He just sat there fidgeting with the Velcro on his shoes.

'. . . Cally and Jimmy.'

Me and Aisha hugged each other in celebration.

Jimmy leaped up from his cushion and cried, 'Woooooo hooooooo!' He almost trod on Nina Wilinska in his excitement and Miss Loretta was doing her best to shield everyone from his windmill arms. She couldn't get him to calm down and sit down again, so she took him off to collect his coat and bag for home time.

 19

It was down to me to listen to the rest of the instructions of course as Mrs Wright explained, 'So, Cally, if you could let your mum and your grandma know that you will be able to take Lightning home with you on Friday, that would be great. The school will provide you with all the food and bedding you need for his cage, so you won't need to worry about any of that.' There'd be a book of instructions to go with it all too, so nothing could go wrong. Surely.

When it was finally Friday afternoon and we got to bring Lightning home there was a big argument over where we would put his cage. Yiayia sleeps in a special room we made for her next to the living room so there was no way we could keep him anywhere downstairs. She couldn't stand the racket Lightning made when he was running about on his hamster wheel. 'Is drive me crazy all this tikki-takka!' she said

when we first put his cage down on the dining table. 'And you can't to be putting mouse here,' she shrieked, 'is where is people eat!'

'I think we'd better take Lightning upstairs,' said Mum.

So then there was the argument about who was going to get to have him in their room.

'He has to stay in my bedroom of course,' I said. 'I *am* the oldest.' Only by seventeen minutes and forty-two seconds, but it still counts.

'What difference does that make? As if Lightning cares.'

'Well . . . whatever. I'm the one who's the most responsible.'

'You're the one who's most boring, you mean. Lightning likes me loads better, I can tell. See the way he's looking at me with his little biddy eyes. It's like he's saying, "Please, Jimmy, please can I play with you in your room? Don't make me go with Cally the loser."'

'*You're* the loser. If it wasn't for me, I bet Mrs Wright wouldn't even have chosen us to look after Lightning. It's not as if you ever do anything good at school.'

'Now, now, Calista,' said Mum. 'Let's not be unkind to Jimmy.' Mum always calls me Calista when she's being cross or serious with me.

'Let's not be unkind to Jimmy, let's not be unkind to Jimmy . . .' I grumbled. 'It's always all about Jimmy. What about me for once?'

Yiayia threw her hands up in the air and cried, 'Mana mou, mana mou! See what is problem this mouse cause? I tell you not to bring mouse here.'

'He's a *hamster*, Yiayia!' both me and Jimmy yelled at once. Then we burst out laughing. We couldn't help it.

Mum was shaking her head and sighing. But smiling too. 'I tell you what. We'll just take it in turns,' said Mum. 'And before you two start arguing over who's going to have him in their bedroom first, we'll flip a coin to settle it.'

Mum found a ten pence coin and Jimmy called out, 'Heads' before I even got a chance. And it landed on heads. And that's how Jimmy got to have Lightning in his room first. So he got what he wanted anyway.

'At least let me be the one to carry him upstairs,' I said. And Jimmy agreed to that. Mum and Yiayia left us to it as we grandly took Lightning up to Jimmy's room and carefully placed the cage on top of the chest of drawers.

We stood there staring through the bars at Lightning. He was snuffling around, twitching his nose and looking about.

'I wonder what he's thinking,' said Jimmy.

'He's probably thinking, "What's that stinky smell?" what with your socks thrown about all over the floor and everything.'

'Ha, ha, very funny. Not,' said Jimmy.

We both stood there for ages, just watching him. Like we were hypnotised. Our eyes following his little snuffly, scuffly journey around the cage.

'I wish we could get him out for a play,' sighed Jimmy.

'You know what Mrs Wright said. We can only do that when there's a grown-up around. And Mum's not going to want to be bothered with that now.' It was already evening and Mum was having what she calls her 'after-work downtime'. And as for Yiayia, well, even Jimmy knew there was no point even thinking about asking her.

'But it's not fair . . .' whinged Jimmy.

'Well that's the rules,' I said.

Jimmy gave me a look. As if to tell me I was being a boring nerd. But it wasn't like that. Lightning was an important responsibility. That was all. And I'm good at being responsible. One of us has to be.

'Tell you what,' I said. 'When Aisha comes over tomorrow, we can clean out his cage together.'

Jimmy seemed to settle for that and so Lightning stayed in his cage for the rest of the night.

The next day, Jimmy still wasn't much getting the hang of the responsibilities at all. When we were having breakfast, he poured an extra bowl of cereal out and made to leave the table with it.

'What is it you doing, Jimmy?' asked Yiayia.

'I'm taking Lightning up his breakfast, aren't I?' he said.

I rolled my eyes, 'Why don't you take him a slice of toast and halloumi while you're at it?' I said.

'Nah. I don't think they eat that,' he replied. Jimmy doesn't always get sarcasm.

'They don't eat Superco's Choco Flakes either, you idiot,' I said.

'Don't to be calling him idiot, Calista,' said Yiayia.

'I'm only saying . . .' I huffed. 'Lightning's got his own special food, hasn't he? Anyone

27

should know that. We can't have Jimmy making him sick already.'

Jimmy tipped the cereal back in the box and sank down in his seat.

'See? Is make upset Jimmy now. Is already mouse makes argument. I tell you mouse is problem only.'

Jimmy was too busy sulking and I was too annoyed about him getting the favouritism treatment from Yiayia, as usual, to even bother to remind Yiayia that Lightning was a hamster. A hamster, Yiayia. Not a mouse.

Luckily Aisha turned up not too long after that, to hang out with us, and as soon as she arrived, we all marched straight upstairs to see Lightning. All of us except Yiayia, obviously. She was very happy to get back to her knitting in peace.

'He's in Jimmy's room for now,' I explained. 'But we're taking it in turns. I'm getting him tonight.'

Lightning came right up to the bars of the
cage and poked his nose through. 'Awwwwww.
Look at him. He's soooo cute,' said Aisha,
tickling his little twitchy nose with the tip of
her finger.

'Cally said that when you got here we could
clean out his cage,' said Jimmy.

'Sure,' said Aisha. 'That'll be fun.'

It wasn't even that mucky but we were all
dying to do more than just stare at Lightning
from the other side of the bars all day.

 29

In his bag of toys was a special plastic run-about ball that you could put him inside so that he could roll around on the floor.

'We're meant to always have a grown-up with us if we want to get him out, but I think if we put him inside the ball whilst he's still in his cage, and then move him, it still sort of counts as all right, doesn't it?' I said.

'Totally,' said Jimmy, making a grab for the ball.

'I don't think you should do it, Jimmy. You'll only end up dropping him or something,' I said.

'Says who?'

'Says me!'

Jimmy started to fume, so before it turned into a full-blown row, I said, 'Let Aisha do it. She's our guest and she doesn't get to have Lightning all the time like we do.'

Jimmy shrugged. It was only fair after all.

So Aisha, ever so carefully, took the two halves of the plastic sphere and lowered them over Lightning through the door in the top of the cage. She then very gently cupped him inside and twisted the two parts together to make the ball. 'Got him,' she said. And we all said, 'Phew,' not realising we'd been holding our breath up until that moment.

She placed him on the carpet and we all said, 'Aah,' as Lightning started rolling around in his plastic ball.

'Shut the bedroom door so he doesn't end up out on the landing. We don't want him rolling down the stairs,' I said. Although Lightning was mostly rolling into the walls it seemed.

'Right then,' said Jimmy. 'I'll go run him a bath while you do the bedding.'

Me and Aisha burst out laughing.

'What?' said Jimmy.

'Ha ha ha. Run him a bath,' hooted Aisha.

Jimmy went bright red. 'I . . . I . . . I didn't mean an actual bath. I meant, like, in the sink, didn't I?' Then he started rummaging about in Lightning's kitbag saying, 'So where's his special hamster soap then?'

Me and Aisha practically fell to the floor in hysterics at that point. Jimmy went even redder. Lightning just continued to bash into the wall.

'Hamsters clean *themselves*, Jimmy! And they've got their own natural oils in their fur. You can't get them wet. It's really really *really* bad for them if you do that.'

'Well, how was I to know?' he said.

'Same way as I do. Read. Think. Use your common sense,' I said.

Aisha stopped laughing. She looked at me.

Then she looked at Jimmy. Then she looked at me again. Maybe I had been a bit hard on him. And it probably wasn't very nice us both laughing together at him like that.

'Never mind, Jimmy,' I said.

'You can do the sawdust, if you like?' said Aisha.

And Lightning just bashed into the wall, again.

That night it was my turn to have Lightning in my room. And I was really excited about it at first. But what I hadn't realised was how much noise he was going to make when I was trying to get to sleep. I knew that hamsters could be nocturnal, but I suppose I just didn't think that meant that Lightning was planning on having some sort of midnight party on his hamster wheel that would go on for hours and hours and hours.

I tried everything – sticking my fingers in my ears, counting the glow stars on my ceiling, burying my head under the pillow, but it was impossible. *Scratch, scratch, scratch* went Lightning around his cage, *trundle, trundle, trundle* went Lightning on his wheel – like literally *all* night. Jimmy's a much deeper sleeper than me. You should hear the way he snores his head off. So he hadn't been bothered by it when he had him in his room the night before.

Scratch, scratch, scratch went Lightning, again and again and again. Fine! Jimmy was welcome to him. I climbed out of bed, lifted Lightning's cage off my desk and carried it back into Jimmy's room. Jimmy was fast asleep. He didn't notice a thing.

Not until the next morning that is, when

he woke up and wandered into my room scratching his head and looking all confused.

'How did Lightning get back into my room in the night?'

'I put him there. He was making way too much noise. You can have him.'

'Woo hoo! Bonus!' said Jimmy.

'To sleep over that is. I'm still equally in charge,' I reminded him. 'In fact, I'm still *mainly* in charge, cos I'm the one who's not going to feed him Choco Flakes or put him in the bath.'

'Woo hoo! Bonus!'

After that, we got used to looking after Lightning and everything settled down. But we still never seemed to get the chance to take him out of his cage for a proper play. Mum was out all day at work and when she got home late every evening, she either said she still had loads to do around the house or else she was too tired. 'Another time,' she'd say. But there never seemed to be a right time. And as for Yiayia, well, she still wanted absolutely nothing to do with the hamster. Or mouse, as she kept calling him.

It was nearly the end of the week now. Soon we'd have to take Lightning back. Time was running out. So I wasn't surprised when I went into Jimmy's room on the Friday evening to find him looking with great temptation at the door to Lightning's cage.

'Jimmy! No!'

'Can't we get him out to play even just for a little bit?' pleaded Jimmy. 'We can make sure we shut the bedroom door. He'll be safe.'

'But look at the state of your room. There's stuff everywhere. We'll totally lose him in all that. Plus, there's the rules . . .'

'You're such a goody two-shoes. Why can't you be more fun?'

'I . . . I . . . I know how to have fun,' I said. Then I looked at Lightning in his cage who was looking back at us. He was sitting up on his back feet with his front paws under his chin. A bit like when Jimmy's doing his begging act with Yiayia.

'OMG, Jimmy, you've practically turned him into you already,' I said.

'Come on, Cals. Look at him. It's like he's saying, "Please, Cally, please, Jimmy, please let me out to play."'

I looked at Lightning sitting there on his back feet. So cute. So sweet.

'Well . . . I suppose . . .'

'And it's nearly the end of half term. This could be our last chance,' said Jimmy.

Lightning started climbing the bars of the cage, gnawing at them with his teeth.

'See,' said Jimmy. 'He totally wants to come out. It would be animal cruelty to leave him in there, wouldn't it?'

Jimmy can be very persuasive. And to be honest, I could easily be persuaded anyway by then, because I really wanted to have a proper play with Lightning too. So, being sure to shut the bedroom door ever so tightly, I turned to Jimmy and said, 'OK. Let's do it.'

I lifted the cage down to the floor so he wouldn't have too far to fall if we did happen to drop him. Lightning can be really wriggly. I opened the door of the cage and reached in ever so carefully. Lightning dashed straight over to my hand and whizzed up my arm. Before I knew it, he was already on my shoulder and scrambling up into my hair.

Jimmy cracked up.

'Stop laughing and get him off me,' I squealed.

Jimmy untangled Lightning from my hair and tried his best to hold onto him. 'He's really squiggly, isn't he?'

'Let's sit down with our legs out and make a sort of circle for him,' I said.

So we did that and Jimmy put Lightning down in between us. He started racing around at a hundred miles per hour and scrambling up our legs so we had to keep putting him gently back into the circle.

'He really is as quick as lightning, isn't he?' said Jimmy.

'Ooh. Get you, using your similes,' I said.

'What's a simile?' said Jimmy.

'Oh, never mind. Just look out, will you,' I said as Lightning almost escaped over the top of Jimmy's knees.

'Shall we get some of his toys out of the bag?' said Jimmy.

'Good idea,' I agreed. Mrs Wright had sent us home with a set of tubes which you could fix

together to make a maze of tunnels for him.

Without thinking, cos he never thinks, Jimmy leaped up to go and get the toys and broke our circle.

'Jimmy, wait!'

But it was too late. Lightning had already made a dash for it under Jimmy's bed. The two of us lay with our bellies to the floor and tried to see where Lightning had got to. We could hear him scrabbling about, but we couldn't see him.

'Get your phone,' said Jimmy.

'What? Lightning's not exactly on Messenger, is he?'

'Nooo. For the torch on it, silly.'

'Who are you calling silly? You're the one who let him get away.'

'No, I didn't!'

'Yes, you did!'

'No, I . . . Oh, whatever, just get your phone, Cals.'

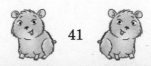

41

So I did, and we shone it under Jimmy's bed in the hope of seeing where Lightning had got to.

'OMG, we'll never be able to find him in all that!' I despaired. It was like a dust jungle of Jimmy-mess under there. Toy cars, crumpled t-shirts, empty juice cartons, ripped up homework, stinky old socks, a deflated football, one football boot, ('That's where it got to,' said Jimmy).'You really need to be more tidy, Jimmy,' I said, trying to hold my nose at the same time. 'It's disgusting.'

But Lightning didn't think so. It was heaven to him. He burrowed in and out of Jimmy's junk as if he was having the time of his life.

'Let's tip the bed up,' I said.

So we did.

'What's going on up there, you two?'

Mum! She must have got back from work.

'Nothingggggg!' we both chorused.

'Quick!' said Jimmy.

We cleared all the rubbish away from the floor in search of Lightning.

'Where did he go?' said Jimmy. We couldn't see him anywhere.

'Shhhhhh, listen . . .' I said.

We stood dead still, just our hearts beating and the sound of our breathing as we listened out for Lightning.

There was a *scratch, scratch, scratching,* coming from under our feet. We looked at each other in horror.

'He's under the floorboards,' I gasped.

'How did he get there?' said Jimmy.

'Lightning gets everywhere, doesn't he? The more important thing is, how do we get him out?'

And that's when Mum came charging up the stairs saying, 'I know you two are up to something . . .' She burst into Jimmy's room and stared at the state of the place in dismay. 'What in heaven's name . . .?'

Yiayia was close on her heels. She had to hold onto the door frame to steady herself when she saw the chaos all around us. 'What is happen here? Is look like war of 1974!'

'It's Lightning . . .' I tried to explain.

'Is mouse do all this? Is mouse turn bed upside down?' said Yiayia shaking her head.

Jimmy's bottom lip began to wobble, 'We've . . . we've . . . we've lost him.'

'Oh dear,' sighed Mum.

'Well, not lost him exactly . . .' I said.

44

'What do you mean? You've either lost him or you haven't,' said Mum, losing her patience.

'Well, we know where he is . . . it's just we can't sort of get to him.'

Everyone went quiet. And then we heard it again. The *scratch, scratch, scratching*, under our feet. Mum's eyes widened in horror as she realised exactly where Lightning was.

'He's under the floorboards!' she cried. 'He's under the godforsaken floorboards. Give me strength.'

'We . . . we . . . we can get him out though, Mum, can't we?' stammered Jimmy, very much on the edge of tears now.

'Well . . .' said Mum. '*We* can't . . . but I know just the man who can!'

Oh, no. I knew exactly who she meant.

'Who?' said Jimmy.

'Why, Grant of course,' smiled Mum.

Grant.

Grant's this fix-it man who comes round to do painting and put up shelves and mend the leaky taps in the bathroom. That sort of thing. He comes round even when stuff hardly even needs fixing. Mum thinks he's some sort of hero. So does he. We don't. Always so full of himself, like he's the greatest fix-it man the world has ever known. Yiayia doesn't like him much either. She doesn't say it, but she always goes all tight-lipped and sniffy whenever he's around.

But Mum was already on the phone to him, twiddling her hair and putting on this silly giggly voice she does whenever she's speaking to Grant.

'Yes, it's me . . . Stella . . . Oh not so bad, how are you?' And then Mum threw her head back and laughed as if Grant had cracked the most hilarious joke ever. But he's not that funny at all. He just thinks he is.

'Well, actually, I say, "not so bad" but we're having a bit of a crisis over here . . .' Mum explained. 'Well, you wouldn't believe it, but there's a hamster under the floorboards!' Mum laughed again. I imagined Grant was being 'clever'. Not. '. . . I know . . . No, it belongs to the school, the kids were allowed to bring it home for half term . . . Yes, well, you know what they're like . . .'

What? Ganging up on us together. Grant doesn't know what we're like at all. He just thinks he knows everything, the big know-it-all! Anyway, it seemed he was coming round to save the day, whether we wanted him to or not.

Grant arrived in less than ten minutes. Keen-o! I watched from the top of the stairs as Mum went down to let him in. She flicked her hair before she answered the door to him. 'That was quick!' she said.

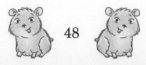

'Well, you know. Anything for you, Stella,' he replied winking at her.

Puke.

'So where's the little rodent then?' he said, striding in with his bag of tools.

'He's in Jimmy's room,' said Mum, leading Grant upstairs.

'Hallo, Yar-Yar,' Grant said when he got onto the landing. He couldn't even say Yiayia properly! Yiayia just nodded her head stiffly and gestured to Jimmy's room, as if to say, 'You'd better just get on with what you came here to do.'

'Hallo, kiddiewinks,' he said as he walked into the room. *Kiddiewinks!* Grant always calls us that. As if he's our pal or something.

Anyway, who calls anyone kiddiewinks these days? Only old-fashioned losers like Grant, that's who.

'So, what sort of trouble have you been causing your poor ma today then?' he chuckled, looking at Jimmy who was lying on the floor listening out for Lightning's scratching and scrabbling, to make sure he was still there and alive.

Jimmy ignored him so Grant got to work, rolling back Jimmy's carpet and wrenching up the floorboards one by one.

'Now where's the little critter? We'll soon have him safe and sound again.'

'There he is!' squealed Jimmy.

Sure enough, there was Lightning, nestled amongst a dust-pile, his peach fur, now a grubby grey, but looking quite cosy all the same.

Grant crouched down, reached out towards Lightning and cupped him in his hands. 'There we go, little fella. Easy does it now.'

'Oh, you are good,' swooned Mum.

So now Grant could add Animal Rescue Hero to his list of great achievements too.

'Just gotta know how to handle 'em, haven't you,' said Grant, acting like some sort of great expert. 'Gotta hold 'em gently, just like this. Give them a little stroke between the ears. They like that, see?'

'I didn't know you were such a natural, Grant,' said Mum.

'Ah well . . . you know . . .' he said. 'You've just got to understand how to— *Urrghhh!* The dirty little blighter!'

Grant suddenly went from mushy to mad. Lightning had only gone and done a number two,

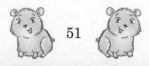

right there in his hands. He shook Lightning off in disgust. Not so much the great hamster handler now, eh?

Me and Jimmy cracked up. Yiayia was trying not to laugh too, I could tell. Perhaps she was beginning to like Lightning after all.

'Oh dear, Grant,' said Mum. 'I'm terribly sorry.'

Lightning made a dash for the door.

'Quick! He's getting away again!' I cried.

And before we knew it, Lightning was already on the landing, then making a run for it down the stairs, with all of us chasing after him in a line – me, Jimmy, Mum, Grant and Yiayia. It was crazy.

'He's heading for the living room!'

'Quick! After him!'

'What'll Mrs Wright say?!'

'Crafty little critter!'

'I tell you mouse is problem. I tell you!'

We all bundled into the living room, closing in on poor old Lightning who was frantically zipping about in the window bay. He must have been terrified. Then he made a dive for it. Straight into Yiayia's knitting basket. Yiayia gasped in horror. Mum quickly flipped the lid of the basket shut and held it down firmly with both hands. And that was that. Lightning was safe. Frazzled. But safe.

'Let's just get him back where he belongs, shall we?' said Grant, taking the basket from Mum and leading me and Jimmy back upstairs. Mum stayed behind to look after Yiayia who looked like she definitely needed a nice cup of sweet tea.

When we got to Jimmy's room, Grant slung Lightning somewhat unceremoniously back into his cage. Lightning scurried into his bed and buried himself there to get over the ordeal. Me and Jimmy just looked at Grant.

'Right then, I'll er . . . I'll be off then,' said Grant sheepishly.

And that was the end of Lightning's adventures with us. We kept him nice and safe for the rest of the half term. And even though that day he escaped had been a bit of a nightmare, me and Jimmy loved having Lightning to stay at ours. But when it was time to return him to the classroom, I had the feeling that neither Mum nor Yiayia would be missing him very much and we wouldn't be bringing home any more pets to look after again for a very long time.

TOGETHER
IN WINTERLAND

It hardly ever snows in London. Definitely not at Christmas. If we're ever lucky enough for there to be even a hint of snow it might be in January or February. I remember it snowed once in March. But that's so rare. Everyone loves a snow day. And no one more than my twin Jimmy. So last weekend, when it was extra cold, and the weather people on the TV said there might just be a tiny chance that it could snow, Jimmy spent the entire time praying to the Snow Gods.

We were staying at Dad's flat in Clapham

 59

and it had been freeeeeeeezing, so we mostly spent the whole time indoors. Me and Dad like to play board games, but they often end up in disaster when Jimmy's involved – especially if it's Monopoly where Jimmy gets in a rage over having to pay out for hotels and then throws all the money in the air and everything turns into a great big row with Jimmy having to have time out to cool down.

We'd been stuck in the flat for long enough for Jimmy to get into bouncing-off-the-walls mode, so Dad gave up on trying to find something constructive for him to do and let him play on the tablet. I swear that tablet's got magic powers or something, cos when Jimmy's got his nose stuck into a game of StreetBrix he can be quiet and still for hours. And Jimmy being quiet and still is nearly as rare as a snow day in London. I was glad he was finally zoned out on his tablet because I wanted to play chess with Dad, which is a two-person game and totally not for Jimmy.

 60

So it was late on Saturday afternoon and Dad was teaching me all about Scholar's Mate when Jimmy broke from his gaming with a, 'Wooooooooooooooooo! Hoooooooooooooooooooooo! Snooooooooowwwwwwwwwww!'

We all looked up at the window and sure enough, little light flakes were falling. We rushed over to get a better look. Me, Jimmy and Dad. The three of us at the window. Watching.

'Don't get your hopes up, Jimmy,' said Dad. 'Looks like a light dusting at best.'

Dad was right. It wasn't falling thickly at all. The snow was very pretty. Like tiny snowbees dancing about in the sky, but the ground was wet, and the snow wouldn't settle. As the flakes hit the street they just disappeared into the road and the pavement.

'Please, please, please let it stick,' Jimmy prayed, his fingers crossed and his eyes squeezed tight. But every time he opened them again, it was the same. A lovely, delicate dancing shower of fairy flakes, but no chance of any sort of snow blanket.

'It's not going to happen, Jimmy,' I said. I was disappointed too. But at least I was realistic.

'It might. It might,' he insisted.

'Oh, whatever,' I said, giving up and going back to my chess game with Dad.

But Jimmy stayed. He stayed there, his nose pressed up against the window. Praying.

 62

Wishing. Willing the snow to fall harder. 'Please, please, please, please, please . . .'

When Dad tucked us up in our bunkbeds that night, the snow was still the same. Falling prettily, lit up by the streetlamps, but no sign of it thickening or sticking. Even so, Jimmy was still praying to the Snow Gods as his head hit the pillow and as we eventually dropped off to sleep – with Jimmy most likely dreaming of snowmen, sledging and snowballs too.

And do you know what? The next morning, it seemed that all of Jimmy's prayers and dreams came true, because what I woke up to on Sunday, was my twin brother pulling up the blinds and yelling, 'It's a miraaaaaaaacuuuuuuuule! Snow! Snow! Snow! Get up, Cally! Come and see! It's snowed for real this time. It really has.'

'Snow! Snow! Snow!'

Normally I'd be annoyed at Jimmy for waking me up so loudly and for being so over the top and I might have said something sarcastic like, 'I think we might have got the message that it's snowed already.' But I was super excited too, and rushed over to the window to see for myself. Me and Jimmy were definitely in on this one together. Especially when I looked out to find that the whole of Clapham had truly been blanketed by snow overnight and thick flakes were still falling like giant fluffy feathers – hundreds of them, no thousands of them, maybe even millions. It was brilliant.

Dad's flat is on the fourth floor so we could see across all the rooftops for miles. Every one of them covered in snow. Our bedroom looks down on the car park at the back of the block, and because it was still early, all the cars, including Dad's, were caked in perfect, untouched snow.

'That's *our* snow,' said Jimmy. Dad doesn't have a balcony or a garden or anything, so Jimmy was already claiming the snow in the car park. I knew he couldn't wait to get out in it. Me too, to be honest. But we needed to get Dad up and have breakfast first at least – although if Jimmy could have had it his way, he'd have been out there in his pyjamas.

Jimmy couldn't get dressed quickly enough, and when it was breakfast time, he didn't even want to wait for Dad to do his Sunday special – pancakes, our favourite. Jimmy just had cereal cos it's quicker. He slurped down his breakfast so fast it gave him hiccups. But he still had to wait for me and Dad anyway, cos he couldn't go out there without us, so it was a bit silly of him. He went back to staring out of the window, but this time every ten seconds he also kept annoyingly shouting things like, 'Hurry up!' and 'Aren't you ready yet?' or 'Can we go now?' And then it went to a whole other level as he started panicking and yelling, 'Nooooooo! They're stealing our snow!' and banging at the window and shouting, 'Oi! Get off our snow!'

That did actually get me running back to the window too. Outside, down in the car park, there was a group of big kids, scraping handfuls of snow off the roofs and bonnets of the cars and slinging it at each other, laughing their heads off.

 66

Jimmy was getting stressed out, especially cos they were taking the snow from Dad's car too. He banged on the window again, 'Oi! Leave our snow alone, you stealers!'

Luckily, they were too busy ducking and diving in and out from behind the vans and cars to notice Jimmy. They were a lot bigger than him. Plus there were three of them.

'Don't be silly, Jimmy. It's not exactly ours, is it? Stop acting as if you're Lord of the Snow or something.'

'But . . . but . . .'

'There's plenty of snow to go round. Chill out . . . ha ha . . . get it? Do you see what I just did there? Chill out . . .?'

But Jimmy couldn't see the funny side. He was still obsessing about the snow thieves.

'Look, Dad's going to take us to Clapham Common in a minute. There's going to be plenty of snow for everyone I'm sure. I mean, just look at it, Jimmy. It really *did* snow last night and it's still properly snowing now. How brilliant is that!'

We wrapped up in all the layers we could find and put on double gloves cos we had big plans for playing in the snow. Stepping out of the apartment block, it was like magic. The snow was still coming down in huge heavy flakes and even though we were in the middle of London,

 68

it all felt so quiet. That was partly because there was hardly any traffic on the roads, certainly no big red buses going by. It had snowed so hard it looked like everything was cancelled – except fun. It was a proper snow day.

We crunched through the deep snow, over to Clapham Common. Jimmy was busy trying to catch snowflakes on his tongue, so he was looking at the sky, which meant he kept tripping up and bumping into things. At one point he went smack straight into a lamppost, then bounced right off it saying, 'Didn't hurt.' We both couldn't help laughing at that. But when he crashed into me, sending me flying face first into the snow, it wasn't quite so funny. 'Jimmmmmmyyyyy! Watch where you're going!'

'Jimmmmmmyyyyy!'

The common was already quite busy with everyone throwing snowballs, building snowmen and making snow angels. Some people had brought sledges along too, but the common's quite flat so they were mostly having to drag each other about on them. Still it looked like a laugh.

'And check out the pond!' said Jimmy. 'It's frozen right over. I wonder if you can even walk on it.'

'Don't go getting any ideas, Jimmy,' warned Dad. 'I doubt it's as strong as all that.'

Jimmy just shrugged, as if that wasn't exactly what he was actually thinking.

'Right, who's up for building a snowman then?' said Dad.

'Or how about we build something else?' suggested Jimmy, 'Like . . . like . . .'

'Like a unicorn!' I said.

'Oh puke. Who wants to build a unicorn?' groaned Jimmy.

 71

'*I* do!' I said.

'Well, I *don't*. What about we do a zombie-snow-monster?'

'Now that's just ridiculous. What even *is* a zombie-snow-monster anyway? As if there's even such a thing as it.'

'Oh, what like there's such a thing as unicorns?' said Jimmy. Trying to be clever. Not.

'Come along now,' said Dad. 'How about you build one each?'

Good old Dad. Always trying to keep the peace.

'What, like a competition?' said Jimmy.

'Well . . . er . . . not necessarily,' said Dad.

'No. Let's do it,' I said. 'Let's make it a competition. I'll totally win.'

'Says who?' said Jimmy, lobbing a snowball right at my head.

'Says me!' I said, lobbing one right back in his face.

Dad was reaching his arms out and saying, 'Now . . . now . . .'

 72

Poor Dad. So much for keeping the peace.

But he did manage to sort the argument in the end by suggesting that we go to different areas of the common to work on our snow sculptures separately. Later, we could go round together and judge which one was the best. That suited me just fine. I'd already totally had enough of Jimmy's annoyingness and could do with getting away from him.

So we split up. I went to build my snow unicorn round the back of a big oak tree and Jimmy went down by the pond to make his stupid zombie mash-up thing. Dad went up and down between the two of us, giving us encouragement, but he ended up spending most of the time where Jimmy was, because you always have to keep more of an eye on Jimmy.

 73

Building a snow unicorn had its challenges. I couldn't really get the body shape right. And the tail kept falling off. And the spike on its head came out wonky and sort of out to one side instead of on the top. So it ended up looking more like a snow rabbit with only one ear, and nothing like a unicorn at all.

Dad came over to see how I was doing. 'How we getting on, Cals?' he said.

I flattened the rubbish unicorn lump into the ground in shame.

'Hmmm,' frowned Dad. 'Not quite going to plan?'

'Not quite nothing,' I sniffed.

'Maybe a good old-fashioned snowman might not be such a bad idea after all then? How about we make one of those instead? Tell you what, we could see if we could make it a really big one. That's what we used to do when I was a boy. We'd start off with an ordinary ball of snow, then roll it around and around until it was almost as tall as we were.'

I liked that idea. So that's what we did. Dad helped me get started, but then had to leave me again, to go back and make sure Jimmy wasn't getting up to any mischief. So I got on with the rest of the snowman by myself. It turned out really well actually. I managed to find a decent selection of stones too. Enough to make the eyes and a big smiley mouth and even some extra

75

for buttons. It's a shame there was no carrot for a nose. And it was too cold for me to sacrifice my own hat and scarf. But still, my snowman looked very friendly. And Dad's tip about rolling the snow around had definitely worked, so that the snowman really was almost the same height as me. Once it was finished, I ran down towards the pond to tell Dad and Jimmy.

When I reached them, I stood there gawping at Jimmy's snow sculpture. I couldn't believe it . . .

'What . . .?' said Jimmy. 'What is it?'

I didn't want to tell him. I wanted to *show* him.

'Come with Dad, and see.' I said, leading them both back up to the oak tree.

I wanted Jimmy to see my snowman. I wanted him to compare my snowman with what he had just built. Because Jimmy hadn't made a zombie-snow-monster at all. Just like I hadn't managed to make a snow unicorn. He'd settled for a good old-fashioned snowman too. With stones for its eyes and big smiley mouth and extra ones for buttons as well. And it stood almost as high as Jimmy, just as mine was nearly as tall as me.

Basically, it turned out that me and my twin Jimmy, who had argued about not wanting to build our snow sculptures together, who'd wanted to turn the whole thing into a competition, had actually managed to make exactly the same snowmen in the end. Twins. Just like us.

'Looks like it's a draw,' chuckled Dad.

'Shame there's no carrots for the noses though,' said Jimmy.

'That's exactly what I thought too,' I said.

'We could pop over to Superco and get some,' suggested Dad. 'I could do with grabbing a coffee as well anyway,' he said rubbing his hands together and stamping his feet. 'Come on, let's go . . .'

'Oh, can't we stay here and play?' whined Jimmy.

'The shops are only just over there,' I added. 'We'll be all right here for five minutes.'

Dad hesitated for a moment. He looked at

 78

Jimmy. 'You'll stay close to your sister, won't you? And you won't move from this spot, will you?'

'Course,' said Jimmy.

'And you'll stay out of trouble?' said Dad.

Those famous last words.

Maybe we should have all gone together with Dad to the shop. But Dad was already heading off in the direction of Superco and Jimmy was already making snowballs.

'Hey look!' Jimmy cried, grabbing me by the coat and pointing across the common. 'There's them kids who were nicking our snow from Dad's car.'

Sure enough, down by the pond, were the three big kids from this morning. Two boys and a girl. They'd made a sort of sledge out of a flat bit of wood and had tied a rope to the front of it. The girl was sitting on it squealing her head off as the boys dragged her around on it in circles. She kept falling off every time they made a sharp turn, then she'd throw back

 79

her head and scream with laughter even more.

Jimmy smoothed a snowball round in his hands and got ready to hurl it in their direction. 'This'll teach 'em for stealing our snow . . .'

'Nooooooooo, Jimmy! Noooooooooooooo!' I cried.

But it was too late. It was already flying through the air at a million miles per hour and it landed smack bang on the shoulder of one of the big boys.

'Shot!' cried Jimmy.

I had to admit it. He had an amazing aim.

The three big kids started looking around to see where it had come from.

Jimmy hurled three more snowballs, one after the after, each one a direct hit.

'It's that little kid!' squealed the girl, pointing at Jimmy. Her two friends turned to notice us too.

We were for it now.

The three of them started balling up snow missiles of their own and hurling them at us. Jimmy gave as good as he got, firing snowball after snowball back at them. And instead of being mad at us, those big kids actually looked like they were enjoying the snowball fight with Jimmy.

'He's really good for a little kid, isn't he?' said one of the boys.

That obviously encouraged Jimmy even more and he started bombing it down towards them until they were all running about, ducking and diving and firing at one another in a great

 81

whirlwind of craziness. And all the while I was shouting, 'Stop! Jimmy! Come back! Dad said we had to wait here!' But it was no use of course. I had to go after him too, didn't I? So there we all were, down by the pond, throwing snow about, till our faces stung with frostbite and our sides ached with laughter.

We all fell to the ground in a heap catching our breath. We'd ended up right by the edge of the frozen pond and sat there staring at the ice.

'Do you think anyone could walk on it and stuff?' said the girl.

Jimmy's eyes lit up. Oh dear. Why did she have to get him back onto that one again?

'Remember what Dad said, Jimmy,' I warned him. Then, thinking of Dad, I turned to the big kids and said, 'Thanks for the snowball fight and all that, but we need to go now, cos Dad told us to wait back there by that oak tree.'

'It's not that far away,' said Jimmy. 'Dad will be able to see us from there easily.'

'So what do you think? Shall we have a go on the pond?' said one of the boys.

'I reckon the little kid could do it. He's the lightest,' said the other boy.

Jimmy's eyes had that twinkle in them.

 83

I knew he was dying to do it. Plus he wanted to impress those big kids, I could tell.

'No way, Jimmy,' I said, pulling him back from the edge of the pond.

'Chill out,' said the girl. Then she laughed. 'Chill out! Get it?'

It definitely wasn't funny now.

'We could use the sledge,' said the biggest boy. 'I saw it on one of them Arctic World programmes, it's what polar bears do.'

The other boy laughed like a drain at that. 'What! A polar bear on a sledge! Ah ha ha!'

'No, you doughnut. It's what polar bears do when they go out on the ice to catch fish and penguins and stuff. They spread themselves out flat for the distributionalness of the weight and that.'

I didn't think this boy had his science facts straight at all, but somehow his daft mates seemed to be going along with it, and worse still, so was Jimmy.

 84

The girl positioned the sledge close to the edge of the pond and Jimmy wriggled onto it, belly down.

'That's it. Now spread your arms and legs out and act like a polar bear,' encouraged the biggest boy.

This was ridiculous. And dangerous too. But there was nothing I could do. Jimmy was never going to listen to me. I looked around frantically for Dad. What was taking him so long?

The other boy must have been feeling a bit nervous about it as well, cos he did at least say, 'Do you think the ice will definitely be strong enough?'

'It'll be all right,' his mate replied. 'And what we could do, right, is if the ice does break and he falls in, then all he has to do is, he just has to hold on really tight to the board, and we'll keep hold of the rope the whole time, so if he does end up going in, we'll all just pull him back out by the rope. See?'

This was getting dumber and dumber by the minute.

I could see from the look on Jimmy's face that he was having second thoughts about the stupid stunt too, but he couldn't back out now. Not in front of his new big friends. I watched on helplessly, literally frozen to the spot in fear, my heart in my mouth, my teeth chattering, and not just from the cold, as the three big kids pushed Jimmy on the board, inch by inch, towards the icy pond.

Dad! Thank God!

Dad was running towards us. He'd dropped his coffee and the bag of carrots and was waving his hands in the air. He'd yelled so loudly that the big kids had immediately jumped back from the sledge.

'Run!' screamed the girl. And the three of them scarpered, leaving, me, Jimmy and their hazardous home-made sledge behind.

Dad looked in a right state when he caught up with us. I'd never seen him like that before. He's usually so calm, even when Jimmy's at his worst. But this time it was different. He was totally stressed out and absolutely furious. It was scary. Scarier even than Jimmy sinking in that ice pond might have been.

'What in heaven's name were you thinking?' he said, pulling Jimmy up from the sledge by his coat and standing him in the snow in front of him.

'It was them kids . . . they . . . they told me to,' said Jimmy, his bottom lip beginning to wobble.

'And I suppose if they'd have told you to sky-dive off a cliff you'd have done that too, would you?' said Dad. Then he turned to me. 'And where were you in all this, Cally? I thought I told you to look after your brother.'

It was my turn to cry then. Great big fat tears, plopping onto the snow. 'I . . . I . . . it's not my fault. I couldn't stop him.'

 88

So there we were. Me and Jimmy. Standing in the snow in the middle of Clapham Common bawling our eyes out. Dad couldn't stay cross for long. He let out a great big sigh and scooped us both into his arms. As we sobbed into his chest he said, 'It's OK. I'm sorry I raised my voice. You just gave me a very, very big fright, that's all. You must promise never to ever do anything like that again. You hear me? I don't know what I'd do if anything happened to you.' And then he squeezed us even tighter. And we stood there, together, with the snow falling silently down on us, for some time.

Eventually, Dad unfolded us from his arms and said, 'Come on, let's head back indoors before we all turn into snow-people ourselves.'

'What about them kids' sledge?' said Jimmy. It was still dangerously lurking by the edge of the pond.

'I think we'll take that with us and see if we

 89

can't find a nice new home for it at the tip some time,' said Dad.

Back inside Dad's flat, it was all toasty and warm. We took off our snow-covered coats, hats, scarves and gloves, and put our wet things on the radiators, then snuggled down on the sofa in front of the TV. Dad brought us giant mugs of hot chocolate too, cos no snow day is complete without that.

The news was on the TV and usually Jimmy would switch the channel straight away because he thinks the news is always boring, but this time it was all about the snow. And the news was extra good because it was saying how it was set to continue for several more days and that it was bringing everything to a standstill.

It was at that point when my phone rang. 'It's Mum,' I said.

'OK, well answer it then,' said Dad. 'But perhaps best not tell her about the incident at the pond. We don't want to go upsetting your

 90

Yiayia, do we?' I knew what he meant. Jimmy nodded keenly in agreement too. I could tell he didn't want another proper telling off. So we decided to keep that one to ourselves.

I picked up. 'Hi, Mum . . . I know, it's amazing, isn't it? We couldn't believe it when we saw it this morning . . . Yeah, we went to Clapham Common, it was brill . . . Yeah, tons of it . . . Yeah, we're having hot chocolate now . . . Yeah, I can see that on the news . . . What?! Really?!'

Jimmy butted in, 'What is it, Cally? What's Mum saying?'

'She says they got an email from the school just now, saying school's closed for tomorrow. Cos people can't travel through all the snow and that . . .'

'Woooooooooooooooo! Hooooooooooooooooooo!' Jimmy was off again.

'Wait . . . Mum?' I said, going back to the phone, 'Does that mean Dad can't drive us and we should . . .' I turned to Dad, 'Mum says we should stay here another night cos it's not that safe to drive and she says is that OK with you?'

'Well, if it's a snow day for school, it'll have to be a snow day for work as well, I guess,' said Dad. He looked pretty pleased about it too. Not nearly as pleased as Jimmy though, who had of course by then taken to bouncing around the living room cheering, 'School's out, school's out!'

I carried on talking to Mum, 'Yeah, Dad says that's all good with him . . . Yeah, that's

 92

Jimmy . . . Yeah, we'll be good. Speak to you again tomorrow . . . Yeah . . . Love you too, Mum. Bye.'

When the call ended, Jimmy stood in the middle of the living room and punched the air with his fist. 'Hoooooorrrrrrrrraaaayyyyyyyy for Snow Dayyyyyyys!' he cried. Then he looked straight at me and Dad and said, 'So this means we get to do it all again tomorrow, right?'

Dad shook his head wearily, but he was sort of smiling too.

'Maybe,' said Dad. 'Though perhaps we could try to avoid the parts where you almost knock yourself out on a lamppost, or try to take on three bigger kids, or the bit when you risk falling through an ice pond.'

'Well, yeah, obviously,' said Jimmy as if he wouldn't even dream of it. As if he couldn't possibly ever do anything as daft as that. As if. Except that he did. And he'd certainly given us all a snow day to remember. So who knew what the next one would bring.

TOGETHER
IN ENTERPRISE

Every year the school chooses a charity for a really big fundraiser. It usually involves being sponsored to do something and there are certificates and prizes for the people who collect the most money, so it's a big deal – our school's even been in the newspaper for it. Jimmy always really badly wants to be one of the winners, but he hardly ever wins at anything. He had a good chance one year when it was for a sponsored run, cos he's really fast at running, and basically rushing around at a million miles per hour is pretty much his main

 97

mode to be in anyway. But even then, it's hard to raise the most money from sponsors, because we're twins, so our uncles and aunties and that always give us half as much each as anyone else might get, cos they can't be expected to fork out double all at once.

Just before home time one day, Mrs Wright announced what this year's sponsored event was going to be. 'It's a Spellathon. Fits in perfectly with our Literacy target for this year.' Almost the whole class groaned. Jimmy groaned the loudest.

'That rules Dimmy out of the competition then, don't it?' Mitch Moran muttered meanly under his breath. I hoped Jimmy hadn't heard. I couldn't see his face cos he was all the way at the front of the class, where he has to sit, so that he can concentrate better. But I could see his ears go red and Miss Loretta patting him on the shoulder. She turned round and gave Mitch a bit of a look. So they did hear him then.

Mitch Moran just shrugged his shoulders in his usual, 'What? I didn't do nuffin,' way.

I didn't want to get teased for being a swot, so I didn't say anything, but secretly I was super happy about it being spellings. I knew Aisha was too, because we looked at each other as if to say, 'We've got this!'

Nina Wilinska was Class Monitor so Mrs Wright gave her the sponsor forms and spelling lists to hand out. Which she very proudly did. There were a hundred spellings! A fantastic challenge for me and Aisha. But Jimmy's worst nightmare.

He stuffed the sheets in his bookbag, not caring that he was scrunching them up, and lined up at the door with a face of thunder. When the bell rang, he didn't say, 'Good afternoon,' back to Mrs Wright or Miss Loretta, he just stormed out onto the playground to find Yiayia. He didn't even do his usual lap of freedom around the AstroTurf.

When I caught up with them, Yiayia asked me, 'What is to be matter with Jimmy?'

'Nothing!' growled Jimmy. 'Let's just go home.'

I waved goodbye to Aisha. We'd planned to VideoTime each other after tea so we could go over the spellings together. This was definitely one thing I wasn't going to be doing with my twin. But just because he didn't want to do it, it didn't mean he had to spoil it for me too.

When we got home, Jimmy went straight to his room and stayed there. Probably sat in his gaming chair glued to StreetBrix.

He even ignored Yiayia when she called us down for tea.

'Is Jimmy to have bad day, Calista mou?' Yiayia asked me.

'Something like that,' I said, crunching through my halloumi on toast whilst studying the spelling list.

'What is this you read?' asked Yiayia.

'It's for the charity Spellathon. We have to learn one hundred words and we'll be sponsored to see how many we get right.'

Yiayia looked at the list. 'Ama! One hundred word! Is a lot. But you is clever, Calista mou. I know you is to be brilliant. So how much I give to you?' she said, already reaching for her purse from the handbag she always wears these days, even inside the house. I think it's because she's started losing things a bit recently, and so she likes to keep things like her keys and her money on her.

Yiayia's too cute. My lovely, kind, Yiayia.

'Oh, no, it's OK, Yiayia. You don't have to pay anything yet. We have to learn them first. And then do the test . . .'

'But I know you is to be getting them right, Calista mou,' said Yiayia.

'Aww thanks, Yiayia. Tell you what, you can be the first person on my sponsor form,' I said, writing 'Yiayia' down at the top of the list.

Yiayia was still looking at the spellings. 'So this is to be why Jimmy is no happy,' she said. 'Is too much word for Jimmy. Is too long word for Jimmy,' she continued looking at the list shaking her head. Then her eyes brightened and she smiled, 'You know, is to be many Greek word on this list? *Arachnophobia*. *Arachni* is means spider in Greek. *Phobia* is means to be scared.'

I shivered. I hate spiders.

Yiayia continued, '*Monochrome*. *Mono* is mean only one. *Chroma* is mean colour. *Polygon*. *Poli* is mean many. Shape has many side. And you see? Number of side shape has, all Greek too. *Pentagon*. *Pente* is mean five in Greek. *Hexagon*. *Exi* is mean six in Greek. *Heptagon*. *Epta* is mean seven in Greek. *Octagon*. *Octo* is mean eight in Greek . . . '

'Yeah, thanks, Yiayia. I'm going to VideoTime Aisha now and practise,' I said, taking the paper back.

'Is everything Greek!' said Yiayia proudly, as she cleared away the tea things and I headed upstairs to call Aisha.

When Mum got home from work, she came up to see us as we were in our rooms. Me, memorising the spellings and Jimmy still gaming, most probably. Mum popped her head around my door and saw me scribbling away.

'Good girl, Cally. Getting on with your homework, I see?' She came in and gave me a kiss on my head, but she could tell I didn't want to be interrupted so she went off to check on Jimmy. I was determined to get those spellings learnt. The truth is, the VideoTime call hadn't gone that well with Aisha, cos, although we're best friends and everything, I think we secretly were each wanting to be the one who did the best. So it all got a bit intense. We agreed that it might be better to just teach ourselves and see how things turned out on the day.

I could hear Mum and Jimmy chatting next door. Jimmy sounded more sad than angry now. So I put the spelling list down and went to see what was what. Jimmy wasn't in his gaming chair at all. He was sitting up on his bed with tears running down his face. His eyes were all puffy. Had he been crying the whole time since we'd got home from school?

I did feel sorry for him then. It's not his fault he can't spell that well. Things get a bit muddled because of the way his hectic brain operates all the time. He gets the letters right, it's just they're not necessarily in the right order.

It's only recently he's stopped mixing round the letters 'b' and 'd'. When you think of it, you can see why, cos they're like reflections of each other, aren't they? I try to understand it, but things like reading, writing and maths come so easily to me, I sometimes forget what it must be like for people like Jimmy. And it doesn't help when meanies like Mitch Moran call him 'Dimmy'. I bet the memory of that had been going round and round in Jimmy's brain ever since home time too. And anyway, Mitch Moran's wrong. Jimmy's not dim at all. He can be really creative and clever about some things actually.

'That's it!' I suddenly realised.

'That's what?' huffed Jimmy.

'Why don't we think of something else for you to do for the charity fundraiser? Something you're good at. I bet Mrs Wright won't mind. In fact, she'll probably be impressed with you doing that thinking-outside-the-box thing she's always going on about.'

106

'But what can I do? They already did running before. That's all I'm good at,' grumbled Jimmy.

'You're good at other things too, Jimmy,' I said. 'Like being kind, and being funny . . . and you can wiggle your ears, and you're a top scorer at StreetBrix, and you can do really cool stunts on your bike . . .'

'What use is any of that?' huffed Jimmy.

'Come on now, Jimmy,' said Mum. 'You've got a great imagination when it comes to it, haven't you? Let's have a think. Now what else do people do to raise money . . .?'

'People sometimes make things to sell, maybe? Like paintings, or cakes,' I said.

'Or they might collect donations from local businesses and raffle them off,' suggested Mum.

'Or we could put on a show and sell tickets!' said Jimmy, getting into the spirit of it. 'I could do my break-dancing act.'

'Yeah . . . erm . . . maybe,' I said.

Mum looked around Jimmy's room at all

the junk that was spilling out of the cupboards and hanging off the overloaded shelves. 'Or perhaps we could do a yard sale. It's about time we had a bit of a clear out. Some of these toys haven't been played with in years. In fact, we could use this as an opportunity to have a jolly good sort through the whole house.'

'But we don't have a yard, do we?' said Jimmy.

'Yard sale . . . garage sale . . . or in our case, front garden sale . . . it's all the same thing. It'll be fun, Jimmy,' I said. 'Like when we used to play shops on the stairs, only this time with real money.'

Jimmy pummelled his chest and clicked his fingers and said, 'Let's do it!'

So, for the next week, Jimmy got really busy going round the house with Mum, collecting up things that we didn't need or use any more, for the yard sale. Except Jimmy wasn't calling it a yard sale, cos we don't have a yard. He decided to call it 'Jimmy's Junk Shop' which was sort of a catchy name because of the alliteration and all, but I pointed out that describing what we were selling as 'junk' wouldn't be very attractive to customers, so he changed it to 'Jimmy's Genius Junk Shop'. He painted a sign for it as well and added 'for charity' cos he said that would make people want to buy stuff out of kindness even if they didn't really want it that much.

'You're quite the entrepreneur, aren't you, Jimmy?' said Mum, admiring the painted sign as she put it out to dry.

'An entry-per-what?' said Jimmy.

'It's what you call a person who comes up with clever business ideas,' explained Mum. 'Although looking at what we've collected so far, it's not going to break the bank.'

Mum was right. We hadn't actually got that many things together to sell off. Every time Mum dug out one of Jimmy's old toys, he got all emotional about it and started wanting to play with it all over again. I wasn't much better at giving things away either. Mum pointed out that I did have rather a large collection of unicorns now and at my age maybe I might be growing out of them, but it was impossible to let them go. Yiayia donated one of her blankets which was kind of her. She knits so much, she always has a few spares in a box that she

 110

keeps under her bed. Jimmy politely added it to the sale pile, but I could tell he was thinking, 'Who'd want to buy that?'

'Somebody might like it,' said Mum, reading his mind. 'It's beautifully handmade.'

'And we can make brownies to sell too. But without any secret ingredients this time, obviously,' I said, remembering the time when a batch of brownies for the school bake sale had gone terribly wrong.

We gave out leaflets to the neighbours as well, telling them about Jimmy's charity sale and also asking for more donations. And people were really generous. Dropping all sorts of things off to us over the week to include in Jimmy's Genius Junk Shop: books, games, picture frames, dressing-up clothes, actual normal clothes, jewellery, tools, exercise equipment, things for the bathroom (one hand-soap and moisturiser set still had an old raffle ticket on it), dishes and other kitchen stuff and a whole china tea set (that Mum said could be vintage, which means really old, like antique) and someone even gave us a fishing rod (which we had to warn Jimmy to not fling around and risk tangling everyone up in). It really was quite a collection. So when the time came for Jimmy to get selling, things looked very promising indeed.

'Check me out,' said Jimmy, admiring everything all set up in our front garden. 'I'm an entry-preena!' Jimmy's Genius Junk Shop was open for business.

The sale went really well too. Almost everyone

who passed by bought something. And they all said encouraging things like, 'What a lovely idea,' and, 'That's a smashing sign, Jimmy. Did you paint it yourself?' Even Mitch Moran couldn't bring himself to say anything nasty about it. It just so happened that Mrs Draper from number thirteen was handing Jimmy a five-pound note, all for an old cushion, and saying, 'Keep the change, Dearie,' when Mitch went by. You should have seen his eyes practically pop out of his head. That showed him.

Even Yiayia's blanket got sold. Candice Solomon's mum bought it. She said it would be the perfect gift for her neighbour who'd just had a baby. Candice was there too, with her little sister. Her sister's not much more than a baby herself and when she saw Yiayia's blanket, she grabbed it from Jimmy and held it tight to her chest saying, 'Blankey, blankey. Me want it. Me want it.'

Jimmy, being the perfect entrepreneur by then said, 'Don't worry, Mrs Solomon. Yiayia's got loads more in a box under her bed. I can do you a special deal. Buy one, get one half price!'

Mrs Solomon chuckled as Jimmy dashed inside to find another blanket. Within seconds he was rushing back out waving a white blanket in the air. It was a bit different from Yiayia's usual blankets. It was very delicately knitted together, with little silver beads intricately woven into it to make perfect 'S' shapes. At the centre of it was a cross made of pearls too.

But it looked very old and was going a sort of brownish-yellow around the edges.

'Tell you what,' said Jimmy to Mrs Solomon, 'I'll take an extra pound off it cos of the oldness.'

Mrs Solomon laughed again and handed over ten pounds for the two blankets. 'Tell your grandma they're worth every penny. She's a very talented lady.' It was a shame Yiayia wasn't there to hear that herself. She'd have been well proud. But she was inside having a snooze in the armchair and had left me and Jimmy to it.

Jimmy's excitement over the yard sale had got a bit too much for her, I think. Anyway, we were doing a great job of it by ourselves, especially as everyone was giving us extra because it was for a good cause.

At the end of the sale, we'd sold out of nearly everything and we went inside to count up all the money. I was in charge of that job. We tipped out all the notes and coins on the table.

'Whooooah. Check out that stash!' said Jimmy.

By the time we'd added it all up, it came to one hundred and sixteen pounds and twenty-three pence. Pretty amazing.

Mum came over and patted Jimmy on the back. 'Great job, Jimmy.'

'Do you think I'll be the winner?' he asked.

'You're already a winner to me,' said Mum.

When Yiayia woke up and saw the mountain of money on the table, she was very impressed. 'Ama! Is a lot. Bravo, Jimmy.'

'We even sold your blankets, Yiayia,' said Jimmy. 'Candice Solomon's mum gave us a whole ten pounds for them. Even the manky old white one.'

'Blankets?' said Yiayia. 'But I is to only give you one blanket.'

Mum's face fell. 'What manky old white one, Jimmy?'

'Candice's baby sister was crying for Yiayia's blanket, so we needed another one. So I went to the box of spares under Yiayia's bed, and . . . '

Mum and Yiayia both dashed over to Yiayia's room, closely followed by me and Jimmy. The box was still out in the middle of the floor with its lid off. Jimmy, of course, hadn't bothered to tidy it away under the bed.

Yiayia made the sign of the cross over and over again and kept saying, 'Mana mou, mana mou.'

Mum put her hands to her face and gasped. 'That's not the spare blankets box. That's Yiayia's keepsake box. It's for all her special things from when we were little. Jimmy, you've only gone and sold my precious christening blanket.'

Jimmy went white. He rushed over to Yiayia and held her hands. 'I'm so sorry. But don't worry, Yiayia. We'll get it back.' Then he turned to me. I could see the desperation in his eyes.

'You've got Candice's number in your phone, haven't you, Cally? Hopefully her mum hasn't given it to her neighbour already.'

'What? The neighbour?! Oh dear, Jimmy. This is getting even more complicated,' sighed Mum.

Things are always complicated when Jimmy's involved.

Yiayia looked like she was going to faint.

'Cally, make your Yiayia a cup of sweet tea. I'll call Candice's mum myself and sort this all out. And as for you, Jimmy . . .' Mum just shook her head. She had no idea what to do with Jimmy.

When Mum got off the phone to Candice's mum, it turned out that she *had* already given the blanket to her neighbour. And things were even *more* complicated because they'd named the new baby Skylar and so they were extra pleased at how it was decorated with such beautiful 'S' shapes.

'But they're gonna still give it back, aren't they?' said Jimmy. 'Mrs Solomon can go round and explain, can't she?'

'It's all a bit awkward for poor Mrs Solomon,' said Mum, 'so I offered to go with her tomorrow to see if that might make things a bit easier. It is our fault after all that we're in this mess.'

'Jimmy's fault, you mean,' I said.

'All right. That's enough now, Cally. I think we can see Jimmy's already very sorry,' said Mum.

'Is OK, Jimmy mou,' said Yiayia, stroking his cheek. 'You no cry now.' Even Yiayia had already forgiven him too. Favouritism, see.

Yiayia pulled out her knitting basket from under her armchair and said, 'Is OK. I make another blanket for baby.'

'In one night, Yiayia?' I said.

'Is OK. I make. I put letter S inside too for name. Is name Skylar? Is unusual name. But I make.'

120

And sure enough, Yiayia worked like dynamite all evening, and through the night, I think, to make the most lovely new blanket for Mrs Solomon's neighbour's baby. She even found some silver beads and little pearls to work into the pattern too.

And so the next day, Mum went with Mrs Solomon to sort everything out. Yiayia insisted on going along too, which meant me and Jimmy went as well, cos they didn't want to leave us home alone.

Jimmy was a bit nervous and embarrassed because he was the whole cause of the entire mix-up. But he didn't need to be, because Mrs Solomon's neighbour said that she totally understood and she absolutely loved Yiayia's replacement blanket. She brought baby Skylar to the door in her pram so we could see her. She was fast asleep so we all whispered 'Oooh' and 'Aaah' ever so quietly. Skylar's mum swapped the blankets over and when she tucked the new blanket around the baby, Skylar let out a little contented snuffle. And we all said, 'Aaah' again. 'She likes it, see?' said Skylar's mum. And so the original christening blanket was returned to Yiayia and it went safely back in her special memories box. Phew!

Back at school, when it was time for the spelling test, Jimmy was excused. He went out with Miss Loretta to the computer room to do word games in there instead. And when Mitch Moran was about to pipe up about it being unfair or something, Mrs Wright wouldn't hear of it. She explained that because Jimmy had gone to such an impressive effort for the charity fundraiser with his yard sale, he'd already made plenty contribution enough thank you very much.

Nina Wilinska went around the class grandly handing out the Spellathon test sheets. Mrs Wright commanded us to be silent and to keep our work to ourselves, and everyone hunched over their paper and shielded it with their arms, and then Mrs Wright began . . . 'Arachnophobia . . . a-rach-no-pho-bi-a . . . the word is, arachnophobia . . .'

Me and Aisha looked at each other. We gave each other a sort of smile. Then put our heads down and got on with it. My heart was beating fast. It was so quiet in that room, all you could hear was the clock *tick-tick-ticking* and people's pencils scratching, which only added to the nerves.

Mrs Wright continued calling out the spellings, one by one, all the way through the list. It was exhausting. Even for me, and I'm on the top table. But when she got to the polygons, I remembered Yiayia going on about everything being Greek and how she wouldn't stop saying all the numbers and my heart felt like laughing a bit at that point and it stopped hammering in my chest so much.

When we got to the end, the whole class heaved a great big sigh of relief. It was over. At last. I looked at Aisha. She looked at me. We gave each other a sort of smile again. We must have both done well. But as for who'd got the most right, we'd have to wait and see. Nina Wilinska went round collecting up the papers. Mrs Wright would take them home to mark that evening and we'd find out tomorrow how we did.

I hoped I'd got them all right. I really, really, really wanted to get 100%. But all the way

home something was bothering me that I'd got one wrong. It niggled and niggled at my brain. It was telling me, 'You got one wrong, you got one wrong, you definitely got one wrong.' So when I got home, I checked the list. And it was true. It was *icosahedron*. A Greek word! Yiayia would be so disappointed in me. I was so upset, that when I started checking all the other words to see if I'd got them right or not as well, I started doubting myself and got in such a muddle that I couldn't remember what I'd done for real in the test at all. So who knew what my final score would be.

Dad phoned me that night to see how I'd got on. 'I don't know, Dad,' I told him. 'I think I got some wrong. I know I got *icosahedron* wrong anyway, because Yiayia says *icosi* for twenty, so I put an *i* in the middle instead of an *a*. And I think there were a few more that I didn't get right, because even though I'd practised and practised, it was really stressful so I must have made some mistakes cos of all the pressure and it's really hard to do a whole hundred difficult spellings all in one go . . .'

Dad told me to calm down and not to beat myself up about it so much. He said that no one would expect anyone to get 100% and that I had surely done really well and that whatever I scored, he was mega proud of me anyway. So I felt much better after that. Dad's the best.

It seemed like forever waiting for the next day to arrive. I could hardly sleep that night. But when we were back at school, the next morning, and Mrs Wright had taken the register, she reached for the pile of marked tests to tell us the results. Nina jumped straight up, ready to do her monitor duty again, but Mrs Wright said, 'It's OK, Nina. I'll give these out today. I'll be announcing the top three, but I'd prefer it if everyone else kept their scores to themselves.

We're all working at different levels and it's the taking part that counts.'

It's the taking part that counts. Grown-ups always say that, don't they? Who was she kidding? I wanted to *win*. And so did Aisha.

Mrs Wright went down the list, 'In third place, with a very impressive ninety-one out of a hundred, is Candice Solomon.'

Jimmy shouted out, 'Whoa! That's siiiiiiick!' and the whole class exploded into a round of applause. I was really happy for Candice, cos she's my friend. When the clapping finally died down, Mrs Wright got ready to announce who'd taken second place. I prayed it would be Aisha so that the winner would then have to be me.

But it wasn't Aisha. And it wasn't me either. It was Joshua Barnes who came second, with a score of ninety-five. I couldn't believe it. That would mean that one of us, out of me and Aisha, hadn't even made the top three. How could that be?

Everyone clapped hard for Joshua as well but when they stopped, all eyes were on me and Aisha.

'And now . . .' began Mrs Wright once more, 'as for first place . . . and this is super super impressive . . .'

The whole class held their breath. Jimmy started doing a drumroll on his knees and Miss Loretta had to give him a glare to get him to stop.

I looked at Aisha. Aisha looked at me.

'Let's give a great big round of applause to our joint winners, Aisha and Cally!' declared Mrs Wright. 'They both scored ninety-nine. Absolutely fantastic. Well done!'

Me and Aisha stared at each other open-mouthed, our eyes popping out of our heads, then we gave each other a great big hug and jumped up and down and round and round in circles. It's the sort of thing Jimmy would normally do, but we were that happy.

'Yesssssssssssssssssss!' cried Jimmy, punching

the air. 'That's my sister, that's my sister,' he said. Everyone was whooping and cheering for us. It felt brilliant. Who knew that geeky old spellings could actually gain so much respect.

'Yessssssssssssssssss!'

Mrs Wright gave out the rest of the papers and explained that we would need to collect the sponsorship money and bring it in, then Mr Matthews, the head teacher, would announce in Certificates Assembly who had raised the most. I hadn't nearly made as much money in sponsors as Jimmy had done with his yard sale, but that didn't matter. I'd got the most spellings. And so had Aisha. So we could still be best friends. Thank goodness.

The following week began with a typical Monday morning, with the usual mad dash to get out of the door, juggling with book bags, musical instruments, packed lunches, and Yiayia wrestling with Jimmy's hair and a comb that wouldn't seem to go through it, and we also had to remember to take in our money for the charity fundraiser. Mine was safely sealed in an envelope. I'd collected fifty pounds in total.

Uncle Loukas had sponsored me twenty pence per spelling, not realising there were so many of them, so he had to pay me nineteen pounds eighty. 'How much?!' he said jokingly over the phone when I told him. But I knew he didn't mind really cos Uncle Loukas is the kindest. He just told me to get it from my mum and he'd do a bank transfer to pay her back. He even said to round it up to twenty pounds!

I gave my envelope with the fifty pounds to Yiayia to look after and she safely tucked it away in the handbag she always has on her. Jimmy's money was in a special cash box. Because it was from the yard sale, rather than sponsors, there was loads of change. We'd organised it into those proper plastic pouches that real bankers use to bag up coins. Jimmy let me take charge of that because I'm better at maths. It had been lots of fun. The cash box was quite heavy because there was one hundred and sixteen pounds and twenty-three pence inside it.

'Put money box in trolley please, Jimmy. I look after it for you till we get to school,' said Yiayia.

'No, Yiayia, I wanna carry it,' Jimmy insisted.

We were late enough getting out of the house as it was and so Yiayia didn't have the energy to battle with him over that one too. Worse still, when we finally did get out of the front door, it was only pouring with rain as well. So we had to go back for our umbrellas. But even then, the rain was lashing down so much that we were getting soaked.

'Shall we get the bus, Yiayia?' I suggested, even though school's not that far and we have Walk to School Week to remind us not to be so lazy. Plus it's good for Jimmy to use up some of his energy on the way to school by walking, or hopping or skipping or bouncing, which is more his style.

But this time the weather was so awful it

really was quite acceptable to take the bus instead. Luckily the 267 was already coming up the road so it made sense to hop on. Jimmy and Yiayia then had the same argument that they always have when we get on the bus, where Jimmy wants to sit on the top deck and Yiayia says it's not worth it because it's only a short way.

Jimmy scrambled up the stairs, even without Yiayia's permission, but she gave in as usual. I stayed with Yiayia. I didn't want to be with Jimmy anyway. There was no escaping him though, cos we could still see him on the CCTV screen, and whenever it switched to Jimmy he pulled a silly face at the camera. So annoying.

When we reached our stop, we had to yell up the stairs for Jimmy to come down again. 'Hurry up, Jimmy! We're here already!' He came clambering down the stairs, making a right racket, and we all piled off, the doors beeping and closing behind us.

'Where's your cash box, Jimmy?!' I said in horror. He was standing there empty handed. He'd only gone and left it on the bus.

Jimmy stared after the bus as it trundled off down the road. He reached out his arms and cried,

'Nooooooooooooooooo!'

Then he went racing off after it. Trying to catch it. He almost reached it actually when it got to the next stop. But the bus pulled away again just before he got there too. Me and Yiayia were running behind, trying to keep up with him. It was a struggle with all our book bags and packed-lunch boxes and umbrellas and all.

'Stop, Jimmy! Come back, Jimmy!' We yelled after him. But he kept going all the way to the next stop. Eventually he had to give up, though, as even with all the traffic, the bus was way ahead of him now. Jimmy fell to his knees and punched the ground as the bus disappeared into town.

When we reached him, all three of us were puffed out and in a right state and Jimmy's face was streaming with tears.

'It's all gone. All that money from the sale . . .' he sobbed.

I did feel sorry for him then. He *had* been careless to leave the cash box on the bus and too stubborn to let Yiayia look after it in the first place, but he didn't deserve to lose it, after all that hard work. And it really was a lot of money. One hundred and sixteen pounds and twenty-three pence!

'Come on, Jimmy. Let's go to school. Maybe Miss Loretta can help us find the number for

Lost Property at the bus garage or something,' I suggested.

'We'll never get it back!' he wailed. 'Who's going to hand that in?'

Yiayia put her arms around Jimmy and gave him a big squeeze. 'Come on, Jimmy mou. Some people is to be good, honest people. Somebody is to find it for you.'

'No they won't. It's gone forever,' he wailed.

'What would *you* do, Jimmy? If you found all that money on the bus? Would you keep it to yourself?' I said. 'It might be tempting, but I'd feel well guilty if I did that.'

Jimmy stopped crying and looked at me, 'Do you really think . . .? Like if we asked Miss Loretta to phone up . . .? We might . . .?' And then Jimmy was running off again, but this time in the direction of our school shouting, 'Come on. Let's go. We need to get to school. Now!'

Mrs Wright was waiting at the door to the classroom letting everyone in as they arrived,

rather than making us line up outside, cos it was raining. When she saw me, Jimmy and Yiayia turning up looking all shambolic, she raised an eyebrow, but wasn't exactly surprised. She was quite used to it, especially when Jimmy was at the centre of it all, with a face full of tears and a nose that needed a good wipe.

'Oh dear, what sort of a morning have we had today then, hmm?' she asked.

'I lost all my money on the bus. I ran after it but I couldn't get it. One hundred and sixteen pounds and twenty-three pence. We have to get it back. Can we phone up the Lost Property?' wheezed Jimmy.

'Let's slow down a bit now, Jimmy. Deep breaths. That's it,' said Mrs Wright. She looked over her shoulder and signalled to Miss Loretta. 'Now let's get inside and wash that face, and Miss Loretta will see what she can do to help. How about that then?'

Miss Loretta led Jimmy inside, whilst he went over the whole thing again with her, 'It was raining. So we got the bus. And I went upstairs. And I must have left it on the back seat. Where I was sitting. And then Yiayia and Cally were shouting at me to hurry up . . .' Typical of Jimmy to always try to blame someone else.

Mrs Wright shook her head and sighed. 'Say goodbye to your grandma, Cally. She looks like

138

she could do with getting back home and putting her feet up.'

Yiayia smiled, and then she remembered my envelope in her bag. She took it out and handed it over to me. I gave it proudly to Mrs Wright. 'It's my charity money in there. Fifty pounds.'

'Oh that's smashing, Cally. Thank you. And well done again. Now, let's get you inside too and out of that wet coat.'

When I went in, Jimmy was at the sink, washing his face and still going on about needing to get his money back, 'Do you know where the buses end up? Is it at a garage? Is there a phone number for it? Can we find it on the internet?'

Miss Loretta just about managed to get a question of her own in too, 'So, Jimmy, did you label the box? Perhaps if it has the name of the school on it, it will find its way back to us.'

'Well I writ my name on it. Jimmy George. And our class. 5W. But not the name of the school.' He stamped his foot in frustration.

'I didn't know we had to do *that*. No one told me.'

'It's all right, Jimmy. It's good that it has your name on it. I'm sure that will help a lot. Come on, let's go to the computer room and see if we can sort this out,' she said, leading Jimmy out of the classroom and leaving the rest of us in peace, at last.

Jimmy and Miss Loretta were gone for more than half an hour, so we'd had the register and were well into our maths lesson by the time they came back. Jimmy burst into the room with his hands in the air crying, 'Victorrrrrryyyyyyyyyy!'

They must have found it then. Thank goodness! I was really pleased for Jimmy.

Jimmy was busy telling everyone the full story. 'And so we found the number for Lost Property and then Miss Loretta phoned up, but then we had to keep pressing all these different numbers to go through to all these different departments, and then we went on hold for ages and they played this rubbish music . . . But then,

140

finally, somebody spoke to us and we told them all about the cash box and how it had my name on it and 5W, and had anyone handed it in . . .? And they said YES! They had it. Somebody from the secondary school found it on the back seat on the top deck, that's where I was sitting, and they gave it to the driver. And I told them it had one hundred and sixteen pounds and twenty-three pence in it and was it all still there? And they said they didn't have time to count it but it looked like it. So, even teenagers from the secondary school can be honest, like my Yiayia said, and they handed it all in and they didn't even spend any of it on themselves.'

Jimmy stopped and finally breathed and everyone clapped their hands and everything was all right again.

★

In Certificates Assembly at the end of the week, Mr Matthews officially gave out the awards to the winners of the Spellathon and also to the children who had raised the most sponsorship money. The top three spellers from each year group all got to stand up at the front and shake Mr Matthews' hand. And me and Aisha got a special bonus medal for being the top scorers out of the whole school. We even beat Year Six. So I didn't mind it when Mr Matthews announced that Jimmy was the winning fundraiser.

It had to be Jimmy really. After all that effort. And all that trouble. And nearly selling Mum's treasured christening blanket off to Candice Solomon's mum's neighbour. And almost losing one hundred and sixteen pounds and twenty-three pence on the bus. He needed more than a certificate and a pat on the back for that. He needed a great big massive round of applause. And that's what we got as Mr Matthews said, 'Please put your hands together for our winners,' and the whole hall exploded with the most epic round of whoops, cheers and clapping ever. I looked at Jimmy and Jimmy looked at me. He was grinning from ear to ear, and I was beaming with pride. It had all somehow been very much worth it.

TOGETHER IN PERIL

'Hoooooorrrrraaaaaayyyyyyy! It's todayyyyy!'

Jimmy had been jumping around the house 'woo hoo-ing', extra annoyingly, the whole morning whilst me and Yiayia were busy getting things ready for our day out. It was Saturday and we were going to Escapade Park. The best theme park ever. Well, the best one we can get to by bus with Yiayia, anyway. Mum wasn't coming. She was going for a reunion lunch with some of her old school friends. I hope me and Aisha get to do things like that when we're grown up.

We were packing our picnic in Yiayia's trolley,

147

the usual Yiayia special, including spanakopita, tiropita and koulourakia. We always take our own food cos those parks are so expensive, Mum says. Luckily we'd got a two-for-one voucher from Superco for the tickets, which is handy when you're a twin, and they do a special price for old-age people like Yiayia. But there's no way we're ever allowed to buy extra stuff like lunch at Escapade Park. It's all junk food anyway, which isn't exactly good for anyone, but it's extra bad for Jimmy. It makes him hyper. And he was already in extreme turbo mode with all the excitement about the day ahead.

Jimmy was planning on going on all the scary rides this time. Last year we still weren't tall enough. But we're ten now and have got bigger. Jimmy found this great big stick and keeps measuring us against it like they do at the entrance to the rides. Annoyingly. To be honest, I'm not too keen on rollercoasters. They look terrifying to me. There's this one at

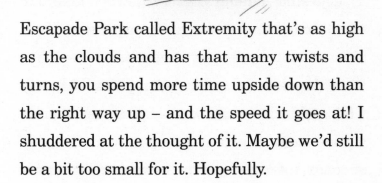

Escapade Park called Extremity that's as high as the clouds and has that many twists and turns, you spend more time upside down than the right way up – and the speed it goes at! I shuddered at the thought of it. Maybe we'd still be a bit too small for it. Hopefully.

When we arrived at Escapade Park, there was no avoiding Extremity though. You could see bits of track looping and curling over the tops of everything else, and every now and then you'd get a glimpse of a cart hurtling by – a trail of screams streaming through the sky along with it.

GULP!

'Wooo hooo! We're totally going on that,' cheered Jimmy.

'Maybe later. Save the best till last, Jimmy?' I suggested, hoping that with the queues for everything being so long, we might run out of time and not have to go on it at all.

We made our way through the ticket barriers and grabbed a map each. Jimmy opened his upside down, then gave up on it after two seconds, taking Yiayia by the arm and dragging her into the park, randomly rushing over to whatever caught his attention first.

'Slow down, Jimmy! We need to look at the map properly and make a plan,' I said.

'Oh, stop being such a swot. We're not at school now, you know. Let's just have some fun,' said Jimmy, tearing off, with me and Yiayia trying our best to keep up with him.

Jimmy led us to a ride called the Fright Freight Express which was basically a ghost train.

'Do we have to go on that, Jimmy?' I said, noticing a giant spider hanging over the

150

archway to the entrance to the station. I really don't like spiders.

'Don't tell me you're even scared of that, now, Cally,' said Jimmy. 'You *do* know it's made of plastic? I'm not scared of nothing. Come on, let's go inside. There's hardly even any queue for this one.'

So in we went. It was one of those rides with individual carts that only fit two people in them.

'Is OK,' said Yiayia. 'You be go just you, Cally and Jimmy. I wait for you here.'

I didn't want to go with Jimmy. He was being way too annoying. Right then he was squaring up to a giant mummy that was guarding the barriers saying, 'Yeah, yeah, Mr Bandages, I ain't afraid of you.'

'Come with me, Yiayia. I want to sit with you. Jimmy can go on his own if he's so brave.'

Yiayia looked at her trolley, 'But who is to look after this?'

'Oh that's no problem, Grandma,' said the

man in charge of getting people onto the ride, 'we can put it safely here on the other side of the track. You can collect it at the end.'

'He is nice man, isn't it?' said Yiayia, as he helped her with her things and then gave her his arm for support whilst she carefully climbed into the cart. I got in next to her. There were seatbelts that we could loosely clip over us, but it wasn't a fast ride, so we weren't clamped in too tightly. Jimmy had already leaped into the cart in front and was raring to go. His cart crunched into action with a jolt and trundled off ahead of us. I could hear him whooping away into the dark tunnel. A couple of seconds later, our cart jerked and jolted off too.

Actually, compared to proper scary things, the Fright Freight Express was no big deal at all. It really was quite plasticky. I could hear Jimmy taking on the pop-up vampires and skeletons, shouting things like, 'You're a fake,' and, 'Wooooo to you too, ghostie.' We weren't that far behind him, and sometimes the carts came to a stop and then we could see him too.

His cart had just pulled up in front of a science lab scene. It was all lit up in green, with a backdrop of bubbling test tubes and glass bottles and there was a wacky scientist who was operating on some kind of giant on a big slab. The giant was under a white sheet, but then it started to rise up and Jimmy – stupid, silly, naughty, reckless Jimmy – was actually climbing up in his cart to get a closer look.

On realising who, or what, the monster creation was, he started raising his fists and jeering, 'Yeah, put 'em up, Frankie!'

He'd got himself right up and was hovering over the edge now, obviously he hadn't kept his seatbelt on. But then, the cart jolted and jerked to get back on the move again, and that's when Jimmy went tumbling headfirst out onto the side of the track. The cart whooshed off without him, and the science lab scene went in reverse, re-setting itself for the next cart. Ours.

We pulled up in front of the wacky scientist and my crazy brother. Yiayia leaned over the side of our cart, grabbed Jimmy by the belt of his trousers and dragged him
in to sit with us.

It was a real squash, but at least the rest of the ghost train characters wouldn't get any more bother from him. Yiayia clipped him round the ear and said, 'What you doing? You could to be break your neck!'

At the end of the ride, as our cart drew up to the platform, I could see the nice man gazing at the empty cart in front of us, scratching his head in confusion. And when our cart pulled in after it, with all three of us crammed together, the man was about to say something, but then just shook his head and went to get Yiayia's trolley for her instead. I think he might have thought it would be easier to just send us off on our way than to bother with my twin Jimmy, who appeared to have the word 'trouble' written all over him. Such an embarrassment.

'Where next then?' I said, consulting my map.

Jimmy snatched it out of my hands and threw it in the air shouting, 'We don't need that.

We're going on Extremity, aren't we? It's right there.'

Extremity was everywhere.

Those rattling tracks circling the park. Those carts rocketing by. Those shrieks streaking through the air.

'Erm . . . maybe not yet, Jimmy,' I said. 'Look at the queue. It's way too long right now.' I wasn't even making that up. The queue really was epic. There was a sign that said, *Waiting Time – 60 Minutes*. One hour stuck in a queue with Jimmy hopping about impatiently or swinging on the barriers or singing daft songs or asking, 'How much longer?' ten billion times. I don't think so.

Yiayia agreed. 'Is look like too much queue, Jimmy mou. Maybe let's be go on this thing instead?' she said, pointing at the spinning teacups.

'No way, Yiayia!' groaned Jimmy. 'That's a baby ride!'

I didn't say anything. I quite liked the look of those teacups. At least they didn't throw you about in the sky at a hundred miles an hour.

Then Jimmy's attention was caught by a kiosk selling candy floss and slushy ice drinks. 'Oh, Yiayia. Can we get a Slooshpy? Pleeeeeeeeaaaaaase?'

As if! The amount of sugar and additives that go into Slooshpy drinks. You should see the colour of them too – fluorescent. It would be like sticking Jimmy in a rocket and turning it on full throttle and pressing the turbo boost button as well. Plus they cost a fortune, which is why Mum always calls these theme parks too expensive and why we have Yiayia's packed lunch instead.

'Please, please, please, Yiayia,' said Jimmy doing his begging act, clasping his hands under his chin and gazing up at Yiayia with puppy-dog eyes. But even Yiayia wouldn't fall for that when it came to Slooshpies.

'Is no good for you, Jimmy mou. And is too much money.'

'But I've got my own money. See, ten pounds!' he said, pulling it out of his pocket. 'My birthday money from Uncle Loukas.'

'Jimmy! You were supposed to put that in the bank,' I said, quite annoyed that he'd managed to sneakily keep some of his cash to himself when I had done the sensible thing and put all mine in our savings account like we're meant to do.

Jimmy didn't know what to say to this, so he just pulled a face and copied my voice saying, 'You're supposed to put it in the bank, you're supposed to put it in the bank . . .'

Yiayia sighed. We'd only been on one ride so far and she already looked worn out, like she would rather go back home and put her feet up with her knitting. 'Maybe let's to be sit down and have little bit of spanakopita and drink I bring,' she said.

158

Jimmy was up for that too. It's a bit like when you go on a school trip and everyone wants to eat their packed lunch before they've even got off the coach. Jimmy can eat for England. And Cyprus. Because of all that energy.

So we settled down in a nice little picnic area on some green hills surrounded by a model village. Jimmy was happy enough cos there were loads of trains. He's train mad.

He does different impressions of the London Underground and everything. You should hear him being the Victoria Line. He really sounds like it actually.

After he'd wolfed down three spanakopita and two koulourakia and rolled down the hills ten times, he announced that he was going to the toilet.

'Maybe Cally should to be go with you,' Yiayia said.

'I'm not a baby, Yiayia. I can go by myself you know. Anyway, they're literally just over there. I won't be long,' he said, tearing off down the hill.

Good. I didn't want to go with him anyway. Just cos we're twins, it doesn't mean we have to do absolutely everything together. And why should I always be looking after him? He's the same age as me. Though you wouldn't think it, the way he acts.

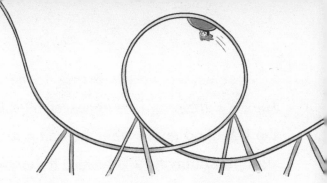

Me and Yiayia sat there for a while in the
sunshine, gazing out at the model village, with
its windmills gently turning and its flags waving
in the breeze. It would have been quite lovely
and peaceful if it wasn't for the wails and cries
coming from Extremity as its carts tore across
the skyline in the background. Yiayia got her
knitting out of her trolley. She always has it with
her. Another blanket. For the christening of a
second cousin's, brother-in-law's great niece in
Nicosia. I picked at the daisies and started to
make a chain.

Jimmy was taking a long time.

What was he up to now?

Yiayia must have been thinking the same
thing because she said, 'Where is to be Jimmy?'

We waited and waited.

161

Just as we were starting to get worried, Jimmy's grinning face appeared over the top of the hill. And guess what he had with him . . . 'Jimmmmmmyyyyy!' I gasped in horror. 'I can't believe you went and got one of those!'

In Jimmy's sticky hands was a giant cup of bright orange Slooshpy. He looked so pleased with himself too. 'It was my own money, wasn't it?' he shrugged, then he took a great big slurp through the bendy straw and looked me straight in the eye and said, 'Aaah lovely.' I narrowed my eyes back at him and folded my arms.

So unfair. And so naughty.

AQUASTIC FANTASTIC →

'Tell him, Yiayia,' I complained.

But Yiayia just shook her head, rolled up her knitting and said, 'Well he is got it now, isn't it?'

Always spoiling Jimmy. Always letting him get away with stuff. He's definitely her favourite.

To be fair to Yiayia, she did at least make Jimmy keep his Slooshpy cup in her trolley and only let him have sips from it every now and again.

'*Now* can we go on Extremity?' persisted Jimmy as another cart of screaming passengers whizzed by over our heads.

My stomach twisted more than the rollercoaster itself, so I went for another diversion. 'Look! The Aquastic Fantastic show is about to start. Let's go watch that,' I suggested, leading everyone over to the open-air theatre which was in a circle around a big pool that

163

had really tall diving boards and platforms for acrobats to somersault off from.

'Oh, we've seen that a million times already,' complained Jimmy.

'Well now it will be a million-and-one times then, won't it?' I said, getting my own way, for once.

Jimmy spent most of the show either in a sulk or trying to sneak his Slooshpy cup out of Yiayia's trolley. Yiayia spent the whole of the show trying to stop Jimmy from drinking too much Slooshpy and failing. I spent the entire show feeling annoyed with Jimmy, especially when he'd had so much Slooshpy that he switched from sulk-mode to hyper-mode and started break-dancing to the music that was meant to be for the Aquastic acrobats.

When the show was over, Jimmy went straight back to going on about Extremity. 'Come on, Cally, we've only even been on one ride so far. And look, the sign says it's just

twenty minutes wait time. We have to go on it. Now!' And he was already charging down the lane and snaking through the barriers that led to the, unluckily for me, much smaller queue for Extremity. There was no getting out of it now.

Or was there? As we lined up, one of the ride attendants came over to us with the measuring stick to check we were tall enough to go on Extremity. I prayed and prayed we'd be too short still, but no such luck. We were exactly the right height. Jimmy didn't even have to try his usual trick of standing on his tiptoes. There really was absolutely no getting out of it.

The man went to measure Yiayia too, but she said, 'Oh, no, sorry, sir. I no go on this ride. Is not good for old bones.'

'No problem,' smiled the attendant, showing her to a side gate, 'you just step through here and wait for the kids on the other side where the ride stops.' The gate was one of those metal turnstiles that only works one way and it was a bit tricky for Yiayia to fit through with her trolley.

'Don't worry, Yiayia,' said Jimmy. 'We'll look after your trolley. We can put it where they keep the bags like we did last time on the ghost train.'

Jimmy took charge of the trolley and wouldn't let me near it. I knew why. It was because of the Slooshpy.

There were just three pairs of people in front of us now. At the last stage of the queue, we entered a dark subway, lit up with laser lights where we were made to stand on these spots in front of a gate to wait our turn. The carts

would grind up the tracks and stop in front of the gates which would then spring open with a clunk. There was this horrible metallic music blaring out of the speakers and over the top of it came a deep dramatic voice saying, 'Prepare to enter Extremity if you dare!' Jimmy needed no preparation. He knew all about extremes. And right now he was going wild with excitement.

Just two pairs in front of us now.

Then one.

Then us.

The cart ground to a stop. The gates clunked open.

Jimmy leaped in and handed Yiayia's trolley over to another ride attendant to put it at the side, then started fiddling about with something at his feet.

'Sit up properly, Jimmy, otherwise the safety thing won't go over your head,' I said, hesitantly climbing in next to him. My legs were like jelly and my belly was turning more somersaults than the Aquastic acrobats.

There was a hissing that sounded like engine pistons and these giant black restraints lowered themselves over our shoulders and squeezed us into our seats really tight. The ride attendant gave them a quick check, and then moved on to the next pair in the queue.

It was just me and Jimmy now.

And then we were off.

To begin with, the cart moved ever so slowly out of the tunnel, click, click, clicking along the track. It had chains and pulleys that hauled us forwards, and then, upwards. The cart tipped

168

back at a steep angle, and that's when Jimmy's Slooshpy slid out from under the bonnet of the cart where his feet were. So that's what he'd been doing down there.

'Jimmy! I can't believe you brought that on here. It's gonna go everywhere,' I gasped.

'No it won't. It's got this lid on, hasn't it?' he grinned, taking a great big slurp through the straw.

Click, click, click went the track as the chain pulled us up . . .

up . . . up . . .

My heart was in my mouth, we were sooooo high now. But not for long. Because after you went up, the only way was down. We were ever so slowly, ever so about to reach the top. We were teetering on the brink now. It was so steep on the other side, you couldn't even see the drop. The cart paused for a second at the very peak and then . . . *Whoooooosh!* Down we sped.

I screamed. And not just from the terror of the ride. Cos the lid of Jimmy's Slooshpy of course had flown off and slushy ice was going everywhere.

'Aaaaaa

'Woo

aaaaaaaaaaaaaaarrrrrgggggghhhhhhhhh!'

The rollercoaster twisted us upside down and the Slooshpy flew out of Jimmy's hands – I hoped it wouldn't land on anyone's head. But I didn't dare look down. It was so high. And so fast. And so, so, so terrifying. I closed my eyes tight and prayed for it to all be over.

Jimmy was having the time of his life.

Extremity whizzed and looped and raced onwards for what seemed like forever, but just when I thought it would never end, it began to slow down. Thank goodness. It was over. Only then did I dare open my eyes again. But only to find, to my dismay, that actually it wasn't over at all. It was just that we were at the beginning of one of those steep climbs again.

ooooooo hoooooooooooo!'

Click, click, click went the track as the chain pulled us up . . . up . . . up . . .

We were at the top.

I tightened every muscle in my body, I gripped the handles till my knuckles went white, I squeezed my eyes shut and held my breath for the steep drop.

Jimmy was getting ready to yell his head off again, 'Here we . . . .'

CLUNK

'. . . huh?' went Jimmy.

Jimmy shook me, 'Cally, open your eyes. What's going on? Why aren't we moving?'

I blinked my eyes open. Sure enough, we were still at the top of the track. The cart wasn't going for the drop at all. The *click, click, clicking* had stopped. Everything had gone quiet.

I could hear one of the people in
the cart behind us at the bottom
of the slope shouting, 'It's broken down!'
'Whaaaaaaaaat!' cried Jimmy.

I twisted my head round, finding the courage to look back. I could just about see the people in the cart below pointing up at us and looking worried. Then an official-looking man in a bright yellow jacket went up to their cart. He had a special metal tool with him and was using it to unlock their safety restraints. He was getting them out. He was telling them to move away from the ride. This thing really *had* broken down!

I grabbed Jimmy's arm. My heart was racing. What were we going to do?

Jimmy patted my hand, 'It . . . it . . . it'll be all right, Cally. You'll see. They'll . . . they'll . . . they'll fix it, won't they?'

'Do you think?'

'Yeah. Or something . . .' said Jimmy. 'Don't be scared. I'll look after ya. Just like when you looked after me when we got stuck in that cave in Cyprus. That was all OK in the end, wasn't it?'

'Yeah . . . I suppose . . .'

That was kind of Jimmy. To try to be the one to make *me* feel better for a change. But still, I was absolutely terrified. I tried not to look down. Every time I did, my head spun. People looked like ants. I wondered where Yiayia was amongst them. How must she be feeling? Poor Yiayia.

Still the ride did not move. We were stuck. Jimmy started muttering things like, 'What if we're here for hours and hours and hours?' and 'What if we need the toilet?' or 'What if it gets to be night and we freeze?'

'So much for trying to make me feel better, Jimmy!'

'Sorry, sis. Couldn't help it.' To be fair to Jimmy, I don't think when he'd planned to go on the scary rides this was quite the kind of scary he'd had in mind.

'I *have* got something that will help though,' he said, rummaging around in his pockets and pulling out a bag of Pick 'n' Mix.

'Sweets!' I said. 'Where did you get those?!'

'Same place as I got the Slooshpy. I still had some change out of Uncle Loukas's money, didn't I?'

'You're not supposed to have . . .' I began.

'Survival kit, isn't it?' said Jimmy, 'We might freeze up here, but at least we won't starve.'

'Give us one then,' I said, diving into the stripy paper bag and grabbing a giant fizzy cola bottle.

Jimmy pulled out a strawberry lace and swallowed it up like a string of spaghetti. 'Yum,' he said, smacking his lips.

I had to admit it, being naughty did have its benefits, sometimes.

Not long after, someone started to call up to us through one of those megaphone type things that Mr Matthews has for Sports Day. Except this one had a bit better technology cos we could hear what the person was actually saying, even though they were on the ground and we were so high up.

'It's all right, kiddos,' went the voice. 'Help is on its way. We're going to get you out of there.'

'Wait, what?' said Jimmy. 'What do they mean, get us out of here? Does that mean they're not going to fix it? Does that mean we're actually going to have to get down from all the way up here?'

'Slow down, Jimmy. I dunno, do I?' Jimmy was losing his cool too now. I suppose there was only so much being brave for the both of us he could do. I didn't exactly want to be climbing out of that thing in the middle of the sky either. Were they going to send a helicopter and have to hoist us out with ropes and stuff like they do in the movies? I hoped not. Gosh. I was starting to think like Jimmy now. I wanted Yiayia. I wanted to be on the ground. I wanted to go home.

The next thing we heard were sirens.

'The Fire Brigade!' I cried. 'It must be!'

'Whaaaaaaaaat?! This thing's on fire now as well!' exclaimed Jimmy.

'No, silly. They don't just put out fires. They get people out of places too, don't they? Like cats stuck up trees . . .' although Extremity was taller than any tree I'd seen. No ladder would reach up to where we were. Anyway, I wouldn't have wanted to have to climb down a ladder from all the way up there. How *would* they get us down?

The next sound we heard was something like a machine. I dared myself to look down over the edge of the cart. And what did I see?

'OMG, Jimmy. Look! It's one of those big crane things with a platform on it.'

Its zigzag frame was unfolding itself and heading upwards. There was a man in a bright red suit with reflective stripes on it too. A fireman. He was coming to save us. Jimmy loved firemen nearly as much as he loved trains. So he forgot his fears and started 'woo hoo-ing'.

The fireman's friendly face appeared at our level. The platform that he was standing on was side by side with the track now.

He winked at us and said, 'Lovely view up here, isn't it? But if it's all the same to you, I think we'll get you down now, shall we?'

We nodded eagerly.

'Now let's just pop these over you, to make sure you're extra safe,' said the fireman. He had two sets of harnesses with straps and clips and he began to loop them around us and secure them together – it was a bit tricky trying to thread it all through the original restraints from the ride itself, which were still locked in over our shoulders, but I guessed the fireman didn't want to release those till we were securely strapped into the harnesses. Then he got that special metal tool thing to unlock the restraints like the other man had used with the passengers in the cart behind us. But it had been all right for them. They had been near the ground. We were all the way up here in the sky. We were shivering now and not just from the cold wind that whistled about us.

'It's all right. You've been super brave so far. Think you can keep it up a bit longer?' he said. He really was the friendliest, kindest fireman. Made me think of Dad.

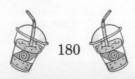

'D . . . D . . . Dad calls us his Twinvincibles,' I tried to explain – even my teeth were chattering now.

'Too right,' he replied. 'Your dad's not wrong there. Not wrong at all. Right then, our Twinvincibles, you just hold tight whilst I unlock this here shoulder restraint.' We held our breath as the fireman fitted the wrench and twisted it anti-clockwise. The pistons hissed as the restraints released themselves up over our heads. But we were safely strapped into the fireman's harnesses which he had also clipped onto himself and the barriers around the platform at the top of the crane he was standing on too.

He lifted us out one at a time and onto the platform. His arms were so big and strong. I held onto him tight. I didn't want to let go. And I definitely didn't want to look down, so I buried my face in his jacket. I couldn't see what he and Jimmy were doing after that, but I understood that the fireman must have been at the controls

181

about to drive the crane back down, because I could hear Jimmy saying, 'What do these buttons do, then?' and the fireman saying, 'You can press that green one there if you like, and I'll pull this lever here and we'll be back in no time at all,' and then Jimmy saying, 'Wooooo hoooooo! I'm the controller!' If only Jimmy knew the meaning of the word 'control'. Oh well, at least we were heading downwards, as I felt the machine steadily moving.

'Wooooo hoooooo!'

As we at last reached the ground, I unburied myself from the fireman's jacket to take in the scene around us. Quite a crowd had gathered, all cheering and clapping their hands. People were taking videos of us on their phones and there was even one person with a great big official-looking camera, like they use on celebrities. And at the front, with her arms wide open, was Yiayia. She looked shattered. Like she'd practically been through the whole experience with us.

'That your nan?' said the fireman.

'She's our Yiayia,' me and Jimmy both said together with pride.

'And I bet she's mighty proud of you too,' said the fireman as he unclipped us and helped us down from the platform.

We rushed over to Yiayia who took us in her arms and squeezed us to bits.

She just kept kissing us and saying, 'Mana mou, mana mou, mana mou,' over and over again.

One of the managers from the park led us to a quiet office behind the scenes. He couldn't stop apologising. The man with the big camera had followed us and was asking if he could come in and get an interview, and the manager was trying to get rid of him, saying, 'I think the children might be a bit too tired to talk to the press right now.'

'Wait, what? Is he from the news?' said Jimmy. 'Are we gonna be on the internet?

We could be world famous!' But the manager was already shutting out the newsman, muttering something about this not being the sort of publicity Escapade Park needed right now, even though Jimmy kept saying, 'I don't mind, I don't mind. I can do interviews. I *want* to be on the TV . . .'

But Jimmy would have to save becoming a superstar for another time it seemed. They sat us down on comfy chairs and got Yiayia a cup of tea with extra sugar in it, which people kept saying was good for the shock. They were going to give us sweet drinks too, but that was the last thing Jimmy needed, especially after all that Slooshpy and Pick 'n' Mix. So they put fleecy blankets around our shoulders instead and called a taxi to take us home so we wouldn't have to go on the bus or anything.

They said it was the least they could do. They gave us all a free annual pass to Escapade Park too. But I wasn't in a hurry to go back there any time soon. In fact, I'd had enough of that place to last a lifetime.

Though, going by my twin Jimmy, I didn't think that day's experience would be the last of our escapades. Cos wherever my twin Jimmy's to be found, there will always be plenty more trouble to be had. And no doubt, I'll be in it together with him.